THE ANGRY TIDE

Also Available in Large Print
by Winston Graham

The Four Swans
The Black Moon
Ross Poldark
Demelza
Jeremy Poldark
Warleggan

THE ANGRY TIDE

VOLUME II

A Novel of Cornwall
1798 - 1799

Large Print Ed
v. 2

Winston Graham

G.K.HALL&CO.

Boston, Massachusetts

1979

Library of Congress Cataloging in Publication Data

Graham, Winston.
  The angry tide.

  Large print ed.
  1. Large type books. I. Title.
[PZ3.G76246Ao 1979] [PR6013.R24] 823'.9'12 79-10638
ISBN 0-8161-6682-X.

Published in Large Print by arrangement with
Doubleday & Company, Inc.

Set in Compugraphic 18 pt English Times by
Marilyn Ann Richards and Adhanet Elias

BOOK THREE

CHAPTER I

Caroline came back to Cornwall in early July, and they had a reunion party. She was better in spirits and less flippant than usual; but she said she must return to London in October for a while, as her aunt planned some grand reception for the reopening of Parliament and she had promised to help. Dwight also, she said, had promised to be present. Could she count on Ross and Demelza? Before there could be any hesitation Ross said of course. Demelza raised her eyebrows and smiled, but commented nothing.

"Mind you," Ross added. "Your aunt is a Foxite, isn't she?"

"If you mean she's at present much taken with the member for Bedfordshire, yes. But I don't think she allows politics to influence her social fancies. My aunt," said Caroline in a pained voice to Demelza, "is a widow, and not yet very old. She is not without her men friends. The present one is staunchly opposed to the government. Ross is being perverse."

"That's not unusual," said Demelza.

"The reception, the ball, whatever it is going to be," Caroline said, "will not take place at my aunt's house, but at that of a great friend of hers, another wealthy widow, Mrs. Tracey, who lives in Portland Place, and whose present friend is Lord Onslow, so I don't think it can be looked on as an opposition lobby."

"Shall you engage a locum?" Ross asked Dwight.

"I'm getting Clotworthy, the druggist. He knows little but he's not obsessed with theory, and uses his common sense. I shall only be gone about a month, and I hope it will serve."

Caroline's eyes went over her husband. "When Dwight comes back I hope he will engage Clotworthy as his permanent assistant."

Dwight smiled at Demelza. "And while you are away, whom will *you* engage as a locum?"

"You mean? . . . Well, I haven't thought — "

Ross said: "Mrs. Kemp can look after the children. She'll be happy to live in for the winter months."

"Oh, I can't be absent all the winter months, Ross!"

"We'll see. Until Christmas, then."

As they rode home afterwards Demelza said: "Do you *really* want me to come with you? You're not just — being polite?"

"Polite?" said Ross. "Am I ever — polite?"

"Well, not in that way, perhaps. I just wanted to be sure."

"Well, you can surely be sure . . . That's if you wish to come."

"I very much wish to come. I wish to be with you anywhere. But the thought of London makes me a small matter anxious."

"Why?"

"I don't know. Just anxious."

"D'you mean for the children?"

"No, no. For all that London means.

For myself, Ross."

"Don't be. You've taken every other hurdle in your stride. Even to entertaining the de Dunstanvilles to dinner."

"It's different."

"Every hurdle is different. This will be much easier. It's not so personal a thing. London swallows everything."

"I hope it won't spit me out," said Demelza.

Ross laughed. "Not if it likes the taste."

"When are you leaving for Canterbury?"

"About the twenty-first. They want me by the end of the month. But it's only for four weeks. I hope to spend all September at home."

"Leaving the children will mean making a lot of preparations."

"Well, make the preparations."

Before he left for Canterbury, Ross called to see Drake. They had met once or twice briefly but not for any conversation.

He found him digging in the garden of Reath Cottage, digging over, it seemed, ground already effectively turned, as if he could find nothing better to do. Sam was down the mine.

Drake looked up and pushed back the lock of black hair which always to Ross was disconcertingly like Demelza's. They wished each other good morning, and talked briefly about the pilchard catch that had come in yesterday.

Ross said: "I'm off tomorrow and shall not be back till mid-September. When are you returning to your forge?"

"Well, that I don't rightly know, sur."

"D'you remember, many years ago I asked you to call me Ross and you said you'd do so after your twenty-first birthday? Well, that's long past."

Drake smiled slowly. "So tis . . . Cap'n — er — Ross."

Ross kicked a lump of the sandy soil with his foot. "I know since you came to live here you've had one miserable stroke of luck after another. Don't think I don't sympathise. It has all stemmed from one unfortunate love affair, but that makes it no easier to accept, nor to tolerate. I'm very . . . sorry."

"Why, thank ee, sur — Cap'n Ross, I

mean. But you must not grieve for me. Tes no one's doing but my own."

"Ah, well . . . I don't think I would agree with that. But I think it's time you returned to the shop. It's nearly three months. You are losing custom. People are becoming used to going elsewhere."

"Yes . . . That I d'know."

"The framework of the roof has been rebuilt and part of the thatching is already done."

"Sam told me. Tis handsome of ee, but I can never repay you."

"Yes, you can. You have money in the bank."

"Tis all lost."

"It is all there. The deposit that you had in Pascoe's Bank will soon be available to you at the Cornish Bank. It will likely not be enough, but you can repay the rest over the years."

"Ah, I didn' know that."

"There is much to do at Pally's Shop still. It will take you all winter. The walls need interior repair. And whitewashing. You'll need to knock together some furniture until you can afford money to buy it or leisure to make it. But the place is habitable now. And while the weather is dry . . ."

Drake straightened up and shook some earth off his spade. "To tell the truth, Cap'n Ross, I don't b'lieve I've the heart to try."

"In that case you'll not be worthy of your sister."

Drake blinked. "How do ye mean that?"

"Do you think she would give up? Or your brother for the matter of that."

Drake flushed. "I don't know. But it is as if the centre of my heart . . . be destroyed."

Ross looked at him. "Do you wish to sell the place? It is yours to sell."

"I dunno. Maybe twould be for the best."

"What does Sam say?"

"He want for me to go back."

"We all do."

Ross looked across at the chimney of Wheal Grace, the top of which was visible over the hill. It had just been re-coaled, and the chimney was sending up cauliflowers of smoke into the still sky.

He said: "Sam has been hard hit too."

"Yes, I d'know."

"But he hasn't given up."

"Sam's religious . . . But maybe that don't make all that manner of difference. Seeing as twas his religion as . . ."

"Quite so . . . None of us can know what another feels."

"Sometimes I think he like me here for comp'ny."

"But he wants you to go."

"Oh, yes. He want me to go. But Sam's always thinking of what'd be best for the other man."

Ross said: "I'll tell you what *is* best for the other man, *always,* and that's work. Work is a challenge. I've told you — I tried to drink myself out of my misery once. It didn't succeed. Only work did. It's the solvent to so much. Build yourself a wall, even if there's hell in your heart, and when it's done — even at the end of the first day — you feel better. That's why you should go back to the shop. Even if you don't know quite what you're working for."

"That's *it!*" cried Drake. "That's it! What am I working *for?*"

"Your own salvation," said Ross. "Not Sam's type at all — though that may come along after: I know nothing about that — but *physical* salvation, on this earth. You worked once to forget Morwenna. And it helped. You worked night and day. Then do it again."

Drake hung his head. He looked a sick man. "Maybe you're right . . ."

"Then when you are you going back?"

"I'll — think it over — Ross."

"The time is past to think it over. Three months is too long to think it over. Will you go tomorrow?"

"I — cann't say."

"Why not?"

"I . . . look, I just cann't say."

"Yes, you can. Next week, then."

Drake took a deep breath. "All right. I'll try."

"That's a promise?"

"Yes."

"Your hand on it then."

They clasped hands.

Drake said: "I'm sorry. You think me

a fool, mourning all the time for all that's lost."

"I think nothing," Ross said, "except that I have satisfied myself — and Demelza — and Sam. And I hope you, in the end. You're too capable to mope your life away. It should not be possible — nobody should be able to destroy a man like that."

II

Towards the end of the month Demelza went to spend a few days with Verity, who was alone except for young Andrew. Verity had seen the announcement about the Cornish Bank in the *Sherborne Mercury* and was all excitement to know what it meant.

Demelza said: "Ross is very tiresome about it and pretends not to know, pretends that it means little. Of a certainty, if you know him, it was not of his contriving! It seems Lord de Dunstanville proposed it at the last minute, after Harris Pascoe's name had been agreed and all, so I suspect he must have had a secret appreciation for the way in which Ross worked so — so tenacious to gain his ends."

"And Wheal Grace?"

"Yielding again, but I think Ross and the others see the end of the kindliest lodes. All the trouble with Wheal Maiden, the disaster, has brought nothing in return. She seems, they say, a dead mine. But who knows? We are assured for the time of an income and work for all. And you cannot tell me . . . But perhaps you can. You are wiser than I am, Verity."

"What were you going to say?"

"I was going to say that if I have a husband who starts a small mine on his own property and, after many failures, it begins to yield big profits, that is one thing. Isn't it? But if you have that, and your husband comes to have an interest in a shipyard and in rolling mills and becomes a member of Parliament and then — a *banker;* that's another, isn't it? Even if four-fifths of his income still comes from the mine, there is a different feeling, Verity. *I* have a different feeling."

"You are quite right, my dear. And

I believe there are other advantages."

Demelza smiled at her and waited. Verity adjusted her cap.

"Of course there are the financial advantages that must come to a man in his position. Knowing Ross, I know he is likely to reject any such advances that may directly come to him because of his position. But they will still come, and one here and there will be likely to slip under his guard because he will feel they will advantage other people as well. So if all goes favourable he should prosper now, whether or no. But I was thinking — when I spoke first I was thinking of more immediate, personal advantages — this year particularly."

"Of what sort?"

"Last time he was in, Andrew told me there was a big concentration of troops between Deal and Canterbury — where Ross has gone. There is talk of an invasion of France. It is four years since any British soldier set foot in Europe. Everyone is very enthusiastic. Ross might be. The more responsibilities he has to hold him in England, the better it will be for us all."

"Yes," said Demelza. "I hadn't thought of that."

And then Verity wished she had not spoken.

During her stay Demelza thought more than once of trying to talk about her own relationship with Ross. On her last visit Verity had seen that all was not well, but her questions had been too tactful and tentative to produce frank discussion. More than anything Demelza wanted a frank discussion; and Verity had such sympathy and understanding. Sometimes Demelza took out Hugh Armitage's poems and read them over. Had *she* inspired such passion? An educated young man, a lieutenant in the navy, who claimed he had known many women in his short life and loved only one . . . Well, that was gone for ever, and she did not want it back, with its pulling at her heart strings, the agony of divided loyalties. But so much waste, to die so young. She had heard people say they didn't want a future life, didn't want to live again. This she could not understand. So far she had done so little, seen so little. She wanted an age, an aeon of life to plumb it and savour it to the last drop.

But she found she could not say anything of this to Verity. Verity knew nothing of Hugh Armitage; she had never met him and therefore would be unable to understand or even guess at his terrible attraction. Whatever her perception and sympathy she could bring no understanding to this. Only Caroline knew and, Demelza thought, understood a little of what had happened.

CHAPTER II

In late August an English army landed at the Helder, at the tip of the Zuider Zee, and soon after an English fleet captured the entire Dutch fleet at anchor and without firing a shot: seven ships of the line and eighteen smaller ships with six thousand seamen who at once hauled down the Republican flag and offered themselves to fight for the House of Orange. Hopes for victory ran high everywhere.

Contrary to Demelza's fears Ross returned safely from Barham Downs on the sixth of September, looking fit and bronzed but with the news that, because of these victories, and in order to rush a militia bill through Parliament, the House was to reassemble on the twenty-fourth of that month, so they must be away in nine or ten days.

Everything then was bustle and haste. Caroline was leaving almost immediately, Dwight a day or two after the Poldarks. Demelza was uneasy that her absence from Cornwall was going to coincide with his and that her two children, if ill, would be left to the fumbling mercies of John Zebedee Clotworthy. Ross would have joked her out of it if it had not been for the loss of Julia.

Dwight brought Clotworthy over one day before they left. He was a pimply, down-at-heel, earnest man of about forty who had come originally from St. Erth and set up in opposition to Mr. Irby, the druggist in St. Ann's; and Dwight, who had had various passages with Mr. Irby for selling him adulterated drugs, had transferred his custom to the new man and had had honest if uninspired service ever since. Honest and uninspired would be his treatment of all Dwight's ailing patients, but at least anything he attempted would come from his own observation and not from some pet theory. Dwight was dead against theory. The followers of William

Cullen had had too long a run. The great Boerhaave, who taught that empirical treatment was all and that one must help body to defeat its own enemies, had been everywhere despised, and the patient treated with ever more violent purging, more bloodletting, more sweat causers, and more powerful drugs. Dwight wondered sometimes if even he did not prescribe too much — often to please the patient — and thought he would be neither surprised nor offended if some of his patients had improved, when he returned, from being treated by someone who had never heard of Boerhaave or William Cullen — or perhaps even Hippocrates.

Ross and Demelza left on the fourteenth. Their coach left Falmouth at six A.M. and they were due to pick it up in Truro at eight-thirty. It meant rising in the dark, last-minute, hasty arrangements and rearrangements, a talkative, absentminded breakfast, then kissing the children good-bye — Clowance not minding because she didn't realise how long a month was, but Jeremy a bit tremble-lipped though putting a good face on it. Then both of them racing off up the hill with Jane Gimlett in vain pursuit, so that when Ross and Demelza reached Wheal Maiden they were there to wave good-bye and to stand in the dawn light waving and waving and gradually becoming smaller and smaller until they were little pin figures and so merged into the background of the pines.

"Oh dear," said Demelza, "I believe I am a small matter distraught."

"Try to forget them," Ross said. "Remember that in twenty years they will be likely to ride away and forget you."

Demelza looked at Ross. "You must've been keeping some bad company."

"Why?"

"To say a thing like that."

He laughed. "It was half in jest, half in earnest. I mean nothing derogatory."

"What a big word for a mean thought."

He laughed again. "Then I take it back."

"Thank you, Ross."

They jogged on a few minutes. He said: "But it is partly true. We have to lead our own lives. We have to give freedom to those we love.''

Gimlett was catching them up. He was coming on a third horse to bring theirs back.

"Between husband and wife also?" Demelza asked.

"That depends on the *sort* of freedom," Ross said.

II

They left Truro ten minutes late because the coachman made difficulty about the amount of luggage they brought, but arrived at St. Austell in time for dinner at the King's Arms, took tea at the London Inn, Lostwithiel, and supped and slept at the White Horse, Liskeard. Including their ride in, they had covered the first forty-five miles of their long journey.

Over supper Demelza said: "I've been thinking, Ross, what you said about the children. I suppose in a way you're right — but does it matter? Isn't it what you give in this world that's important, not what you get back?"

"I'm sure you're right."

"No, don't agree so easy. I mean even if you look at it in the most selfish way: isn't there more actual *pleasure* in giving than in getting back?"

"All right," he said. "Yes. But I just wished you to keep a sense of proportion. So long as you're aware of that — that the giving is all. It's easy to say, but hard to carry out."

"Maybe."

"I thought if I reminded you of the way human nature operates, it might help you to grieve less now at the parting."

"No," she said, "it won't."

"Well, I'm sorry I spoke."

"No matter. I've stopped grieving already, Ross, and am just getting excited. After just one day. And I don't think that's a nice way for human nature to operate either!"

They broke their fast early next morning, crossed the Tamar by the ferry at Torpoint and dined in Plymouth. Tea was at Ivybridge and they slept at Ashburton, having covered almost exactly the same mileage as the day before, though this all by coach. Everybody was very tired, and Demelza could hardly keep awake over supper.

"You see why I travel sometimes by sea," Ross said. "But it improves a little from now on. The roads are better and the hills fewer."

The coach held eight inside. Sometimes it was uncomfortably crowded, sometimes half empty, as passengers left and joined. The only others making the full trip to London were a Mr. and Mrs. Carne from Falmouth, he being that banker Ross had threatened to go to with his friends if the Basset, Rogers bank would not accommodate Harris Pascoe. Mr. Carne had heard of Ross's becoming himself a partner and talked banking a good deal of the time, most of it over Ross's head. To divert him, Ross told him that his wife's name had been Carne before she married; but they seemed to be unable to establish any relationship.

The third night they slept at Bridgwater, having dined at Cullompton and taken tea at Taunton. Demelza realised now what Caroline meant when she said that Cornwall was a barren land. Here there were great trees, great belts of woodland everywhere, trees that made even the wooded parts of south Cornwall look puny and dwarf. The fields were so rich, the colorations of the soil always changing but always lush. There were more birds, more butterflies, more bees. And unfortunately more flies and wasps. She had never seen so many. It was a warm September, and apart from the jogging of the coach the heat was oppressive, for if a window were lowered somebody always complained of the draught. To make matters worse, one of the horses went lame on a stage on the fourth day and they were very late arriving in Marlborough.

The fifth day had to be a dawn start nevertheless, for they were due in London that evening. The road now was the best they had been on, the day was cooler but bright and sunny, and they reached Maidenhead for dinner after a spanking run. The food was good here: a neck of boiled veal and a roast fowl, and a rather heavy but seductive wine; Demelza dozed away the afternoon and traversed the dreaded Hounslow Health without even noticing it. Ross told her that the only highwaymen to be seen were the unsuccessful ones hanging from the gibbets as a warning to the rest.

Great bustle in Hounslow — the hub of the western exits from London: the innkeeper told them that five hundred coaches passed through daily and that upwards of eight hundred horses were regularly maintained here. Ross had never heard this before. As always he learned more on a journey with Demelza than when travelling alone.

So the last ten miles to the city of which recently she had heard and thought so much. The last afternoon before leaving she had paid one of her regular visits to the Paynters to give Prudie a little money for herself, and Prudie had been appalled at the thought of such a journey and of what waited at the other end. "They d'say tis much bigger'n Truro," she'd muttered.

The first thing to be seen of the town bigger than Truro was the smoke: It lay low down on the horizon like a dirty fog.

"Don't worry," said Ross. "That's only the lime kilns and the brick works. It will be better beyond."

The coach entered an area as desolate as any mining district in Cornwall. Amid the smoking brick fields thin sheep browsed and pigs rooted, trying to find something green among the poisoned vegetation. Enormous dumps of refuse bordered the road, some of them also smouldering like half-extinct volcanoes, others sprawling in miniature foothills, where the waste and the refuse were being picked over by beggars and ragged children with scrofulous faces.

Houses met them and closed round them, sprawling, jumbled, leaning as if about to fall down. Some had, and men were at work rebuilding them. More fields, then a broader, cleaner part, with a few good buildings merging into older, more harshly cobbled streets, with dives and alleys leading off, in which children and slatternly women and mangy cats roamed. By now dusk was coming on, but the evening was very warm and in one street women were sitting out of doors on stools in their linsey-woolsey petticoats and worsted stockings, their leather stays half laced and black with dirt. Some were occupied stitching coarse cloth, but many did nothing but sit and yawn. They shouted obscenely as the coach passed and aimed bad oranges at the coachman. Bundles, supposedly human, lay drunk or dead, and children ran after the coach screaming. At last they reached a well-paved area, but this had higher paved ridges traversing the streets where pedestrians might cross, so that the coach bumped and lurched as it went over them.

So to the Thames. The windows of the coach, which had been tight closed to keep out the smells, were opened to let in better air. The river seemed to have a thousand small boats on it. People being ferried here and there. Ten-oared barges. Sailing ships tacked and lugged, in some amazing fashion not colliding with each other. A forest of masts further down, and a great dome. "St. Paul's," Ross said.

As they crossed a bridge the lights were going on. Link boys were rushing around lighting the three- and four-branched lamps which hung from posts in the streets. It became a sudden fairyland. All the squalor and the dirt and the stenches were swallowed up by the evening dark and the opaque light cast on the streets from these crystal globes. The coach bumped and rattled through fine streets now, but hardly able to get along for the press of traffic. They jolted briefly between a coffin on an open cart and a gilded carriage in which sat a solitary woman with an ostrich-feathered headdress. A brewer's dray, with great barrels swaying and a half dozen ragged boys clinging, followed soldiers marching, while a group of extravagantly dressed riders tried to edge their mounts through the throng.

The coach stopped for a long time to allow Mr. and Mrs. Carne to alight. There were polite expressions of gratification on all sides at the pleasure experienced in each other's company over five days, the Carnes' bags were unloaded and at last the coach was off again, edging its way slowly on to a wide street called the Strand. They came once more to a creaking stop.

"We are here," said Ross. "At last. Just down this street, if you can walk after so long a-sitting. The coachman will bring our bags down."

III

The rooms were nice and spacious, better than Demelza had expected after the cramped inns in which they had slept, and Mrs. Parkins, a handsome, bespectacled woman, did everything to oblige.

They had done seventy-five miles on the last day and in spite of their abounding good health they were ready for bed and slept late next morning. Used to the boisterous arrival of her children each day soon after dawn, Demelza was startled and appalled to raise her head off the pillow and to see by the marble clock on the mantelshelf that it was nearly ten. Ross was part dressed and washing.

"Judas! Why didn't you wake me, Ross?"

He smiled. "Don't alarm yourself. Mrs. Parkins is used to serving breakfast at ten. I seldom rise early myself in London."

"No wonder you look tired when you come home."

"Tired for sleeping late?"

"And bedding late, I suspect. It is the wrong hours to sleep."

"Do you want your nightdress?"

"Please."

"Come and fetch it, then."

"No."

He began to shave.

"What is that, Ross?"

"What? Oh, this. It is an improved washstand. Did you not see one at Tehidy? But this one has compartments for soap balls and razors. You will be able to admire it when you get up."

"Does Mrs. Parkins bring the water?"

"A maid does. There is a tap in the house."

"A tap? You mean like a barrel?"

"Yes. But water runs through wooden pipes from cisterns higher in the town, so you can draw what you will."

"Can you drink it?"

"I have done, and come to no harm. No doubt you found last night that there is always a bucket of water too in the

Jericho down the passage. As well as one of sand. It's the best indoor system I have come across."

"Last night I was too tired to take much notice of anything."

"When I undressed you," he said, "you felt like a long-legged, cool kitten, slightly damp with sweat."

"It sounds some awful."

"Well, it wasn't, if you can recollect that much."

"I can recollect that much."

There was a pause while she yawned and ran fingers through her hair.

"A gentleman would fetch my nightdress," she said.

"It depends on the gentleman."

"I told you before. You've been keeping bad company in London."

"Not till last night."

He finished shaving in silence and tipped his water away into the other bucket. She was sitting up now, a sheet under her arms.

"It's not nice in the mornings, Ross."

"What isn't?"

"Nakedness."

"Opinions differ."

"No, you don't look nice in the daylight . . ."

"I don't?"

"No, I mean *I* don't. We don't. *One* doesn't."

"Well, make up your mind." He was putting on his shirt now.

"One doesn't look nice in the daylight," Demelza said. "At least, not as nice as *one* hopes *one* looks at night, by candle."

"I think two look better than one," Ross said. "Always have."

A knife grinder outside was shouting and ringing his bell, and someone was ringing a competing bell and offering to repair broken chairs.

"I thought this was a quiet street," Demelza said.

"So it is compared to most. You'll be late for breakfast if you don't bestir yourself. Not that it's much to miss. Milky tea with thick bread and butter. I intended to have brought some jam."

Cautiously she eased herself out of bed, pulling at the sheet so that it came with her. Out of the corner of his eye he saw her and advanced on her with mischief in mind as part of her back and legs became exposed. She dodged quickly but one corner of the sheet held firm and tripped her. She went to the floor with a thump. He knelt beside her as she rolled herself defiantly into a cocoon, the sheet ripping as he did so. He caught her and held her, laughing.

"No, Ross! Don't!"

"I'm m-married to a m-m-mummy," he said, laughing uncontrollably. "An Eg-egyptian mummy. They look — look just like you, only they haven't got so much h-h-hair! . . ."

She glared at him from among her mane. She was so tight-wrapped around that she could not even get a hand free to hit him. Her hair lay in a tangle about her face. Then she saw the funny side and began to laugh too. She laughed up at him with all her heart and soul. He lay on top of her and laughed and laughed. Their bodies shook the floor.

Presently it had to come to an end and they lay exhausted. He put up a weak hand to clear her hair away from her face. His tears were on her cheeks. Then he kissed her. Then the strength came back to his hands and he began to unwind her.

At this point there was a knock on the door. Ross got up and opened it.

"Please, sir"; it was one of the maids. "If you please, sir, Mrs. Parkins says to say breakfast be ready and waiting."

"Tell Mrs. Parkins," said Ross, "that we shall be down in an hour."

CHAPTER III

A first five days in London of unalloyed happiness. The city was a treasure trove into which Demelza dipped unceasingly, not put off by the squalid and the degrading, though often offended by it. At the bottom of George Street was one of the many landing stages marked by twin striped poles where you could get a ferryman in red and blue breeches and a red cap to take you anywhere. It was sixpence each to Westminster and the same to St. Paul's, where the great church seemed more monstrous in size and more impressive even than the Abbey, though it was disfigured by the conglomerate of sordid, tumbledown houses girdling it, by butchers' shops where stinking offal was thrown into the street, and by the omnipresent stench of the Fleet Ditch.

The weather was still fine and sunny, and one day they took chairs to Paddington and then walked east towards Islington, with the hills to the north and all the city straggling southward. They went to Vauxhall Gardens and to Ranelagh, and called on Caroline at her aunt's house in Hatton Garden. Dwight was expected on the morrow, and Caroline was full of the reception that was to be held at Mrs. Tracey's on the evening of the twenty-fourth. Seeing her so engaged, Ross wondered whether she would *ever* altogether settle as the wife of a remote country doctor. Yet he remembered coming to this house years ago, when Caroline and Dwight had apparently broken up for ever, and how wan and listless she had been. And there was the time of Dwight's imprisonment when she had seemed only to live from day to day. She needed Dwight, there seemed no doubt. But she also needed a stimulus in her life, a social round, or a mission of some sort.

For her evenings out Demelza had brought the evening gown that she had

had made for her in those early days of her married life, and the other frock she had bought for Caroline's own wedding three years ago, and which she had scarcely worn. Caroline gently shook her head. It might be the perfect thing for Cornwall still, but it wouldn't do for the London season in 1799. Fashions had changed. Everything was of the simplest, finest, slightest. ("So I notice," Demelza said.) Waists were high, almost under the armpit, both for day and for evening. Neck and bust were much exposed but could be hidden or part hidden in a veil of chiffon. Ostrich feathers in the hair, or a few pearls. Demelza said, how interesting, and why do so many people wear spectacles in London? Perhaps they live more in artificial light, said Caroline; but then of course it is rather the fashion. I think, Demelza said, folk would walk on crutches in London if someone said it was the fashion. I have no doubt you're right, said Caroline. In any case, said Demelza, there would be no time for anything to be made for me by tomorrow evening; but aside from that we could not afford,

I should not wish to afford, London prices.

"I'll take you to my shop, Phillips & ffossick. Mrs. Phillips has a number of gowns half made that can be altered and finished in four and twenty hours. As for payment, it can go on my account. I pay yearly, and you can reimburse me if and when you have the fancy."

"It seems to cost even to breathe in London," Demelza said.

"Well, what is money for but to spend? We'll ask Ross, but only after we've spent it."

"I hope I can understand what your Mrs. Phillips says," said Demelza, weakening. "I often don't follow what the ordinary people say. It is almost like a foreign language."

"Oh, don't worry. You'll find Mrs. Phillips excessively genteel."

"That also," Demelza said, "I do not so much fancy."

But she went, like the moth to the flame. Shades of long ago when Verity had first taken her into Mistress Trelask's . . . The homely little sempstress's shop in

Truro with a bell that tinged when you entered and you nearly fell down the two dark steps. This was a *salon,* though not large; just well-bred and discreet. You sat in a place like a drawing room, with silk drapes and lawn curtains and lush gilt chairs; and a woman who looked like a countess who had fallen on hard times brought out a succession of gowns, each one presented and considered separately before being hidden away again before the drawing room could begin to look untidy.

After rejecting three on the grounds of indecency she took to one of a fetching peach-coloured satin, which not only happened to be an opaque material but of a fractionally more discreet design. Before price could be discussed it was arranged that the gown should be finished and delivered to No. 6 George Street "at this hour tomorrow," and that the account should in due course be presented to Mrs. Enys.

"I feel like a wanton," Demelza said as they came out into the noisy street.

"That's just what you must try to look like," said Caroline. "It's the ambition of all respectable women."

"And the wantons try to look respectable?"

"Well, not that always neither. Now I must fly, for there's much still to do, and Dwight should be with me this evening. Get this chair . . . I'll see you into it and then we'll meet tomorrow in the forenoon."

The twenty-fourth of September was a Tuesday, and day broke with a light rain falling. Demelza looked out to see umbrellas passing up and down the street below and to see the patten woman bringing back the shoes she had been cleaning overnight. But by eleven the clouds had split open and a hazy sun, much obscured by drifting smoke, peered through. The cobbles were soon drying. Caroline and Dwight and Demelza saw the royal procession from seats in Whitehall, the gold coaches, the bands, the regiments, the prancing life guards. Because of the successes of both the army and the navy a new wave of patriotism was sweeping Britain, and the old King was cheered the length of the street.

The reception at Portland Place was to start at nine, and there was some talk that the Prince of Wales himself might be there. Ross had ordered a coach for nine-fifteen, which to Demelza's idea was far too late but he would not alter it. She began getting ready at eight, and eventually slipped into her new gown at quarter before nine.

When Ross turned round and saw it he said: "That is very pretty. But where is the gown?"

"This is it! This is what I have bought!"

"That's a petticoat."

"Oh, Ross, you *are* provoking! You know well it is nothing of the sort."

"Would you wish me to go in my shirt and underbreeches?"

"No, no, you must not tease! I need confidence, not — not . . ."

"Port will give you that."

She grimaced at him. "And this is for my hair," she said, showing him the feather.

"Well, I don't know what your father would say if he could see you."

"It is the fashion, Ross. Caroline insisted."

"I know just how women insist. And you, I'm sure, were protesting loudly and saying, no, no, no!"

"Well, I did protest, truly. And this is much the most respectable of the gowns I was shown. Some women, Caroline says, damp their frocks when they put them on so that they will cling more."

"You damp anything, my dear, and I'll smack you."

She paused while he tied his stock. "But, Ross, you do like it, don't you? I still have time to change."

"And you'd wear an old frock to please me?"

"Of course."

"And be miserable all night?"

"I wouldn't be miserable. I'm so happy."

"Yes . . . you look it, I'll say that. Why are you happy?"

"Because of you, of course. Because of *us*. Need I say?"

"No," he said, "perhaps not . . ."

Somewhere a clock was striking nine.

He said: "The vexing thing is, good-looking women look good in almost anything. Or should I say almost nothing? Well . . ." He stared at her. "On longer inspection I like the frock. I think it has a touch of elegance. I am only a little reluctant that so many men should see so much of you."

"They will have many other women to look at. Women who have spent their lives being beautiful."

"And men too. These confounded buttons are hard to fasten."

"Let me." She came up and busied herself at his wrists.

"I think," he said, looking down at her brushed and combed and tidy hair, "I think I'll go in my nightgown. It might provoke a new fashion."

II

Portland Place was one of the broadest and best-lit streets in London, and a line of carriages and chairs waited their turn before a porticoed door with a royal blue carpet laid under a crimson awning.

Gowned and beautiful creatures were passing up the steps followed by men scarcely less brilliant. When it came to their turn two white-wigged footmen were there to open the carriage door and to hand Demelza out. It seemed for a moment that they were at the centre of a circle of brilliant light from the periphery of which a sea of faces peered at them greedily as the hundreds of ragged onlookers stared at and assessed them. Then they had passed inside, to leave their cloaks in the care of more footmen, and to climb a short flight of stairs while a man with a rich tenor voice shouted: "Captain and Mrs. Poldark."

Caroline greeted them, brilliant in pale green, with jewels at her breast that were never seen in Cornwall, and introduced them to their two hostesses: Mrs. Pelham, her aunt, whose escort was a tall man called the Hon. St. Andrew St. John (the member for Bedfordshire, presumably), and Mrs. Tracey, with Lord Onslow. And then there was Dwight in a new suit of black velvet, and presently they moved on and were given glasses of wine and reached an enormous reception room already more than half full of people chatting and drinking and seated and exchanging greetings.

As they went in Dwight had drawn aside and said to Ross: "A word of warning. The Warleggans are likely to be here. Mrs. Tracey invited them. But they should be easy to avoid." Ross had smiled grimly and said: "Never fear. We'll avoid 'em."

In fact George and Elizabeth arrived soon after them in the company of Monk Adderley and a girl called Andromeda Page, a yawning, semi-nude beauty of seventeen, whom Monk was temporarily escorting round the town. They spotted the Poldarks quickly enough but moved to the opposite side of the room and were soon lost sight of.

The Warleggans had arrived in London only two days before and taken up residence at No. 14 King Street, just near Grosvenor Gate, having brought Valentine with them, since scarlet fever was so rife in Truro that he was unlikely to be at greater hazard in London with the fresh fields of Hyde Park on his doorstep.

Theirs had been something of a royal procession from Cornwall, travelling as they did in their own coach and taking twelve days on the journey. In his year as a member of Parliament, George had been an assiduous collector of useful friends, and this stood him in good stead. He had written well ahead to various people telling them he would like to call, and few of the country gentry wished to offend a very rich man with a pretty and well-connected wife. As a result, they had only had to spend two nights in inns all the way.

George was in the best of spirits tonight, Monk having just told him of his election to White's, one of the most exclusive clubs in London. He had also had a conversation with Roger Wilbraham that morning. Wilbraham, unlike Captain Howell, was neither a Cornishman nor in need of money, and his first response to the suggestion that he might resign his seat at St. Michael had been unhelpful. Gladly he'd accept money to resign, he said, laughing loudly, if George would provide him with another seat. Not otherwise, since it would cost him as much to procure another seat for himself as he was likely to receive from George, so how did it profit him? An impasse had been prevented by Wilbraham adding: "But look, old fellow, I've stood for Scawen interests until now. I've no strong convictions. I can just as easy be your man as his. You can count on me." It seemed the easy way out, and George had accepted the suggestion. If Wilbraham should prove troublesome, there were ways of forcing him out later. The important thing was that, so far as the government was concerned, George now had two seats to bargain with.

Elizabeth, though slightly plumper in face, had not thickened in figure yet, and tonight looked at her most dignified and beautiful, having spent most of the day receiving the attentions of the hairdresser who had brightened up the faded fairness until it shone like a crown. As usual she wore white, this time in a Grecian style, light loose drapery over a tight tunic, decorated with gold chains, sandaled feet and flesh-coloured stockings with toes like gloves, fan in gold belt and tiny gold bag containing scent and a handkerchief. "My dear," Monk Adderley said, "you look like Helen of Troy."

She smiled at him warmly and looked at the growing company. "One day, when the war is over, I hope to travel, if I can persuade George to do so. I should like to see Greece and all the islands. I should like to see Rome . . ."

"Do take care," said Adderley, "I cannot bear to hear you say you wish to look at the scenery."

"Why ever not?" Elizabeth smiled. "Who is that man over there?"

"The fat one? The gross one? You don't know him? That is Dr. Franz Anselm, who, my dear, makes *more money* out of ladies than any other physician in London. Do you wish to conceive? He will see to it. Do you wish *not* to conceive, or to lose that which you *have* conceived? He will see to that also. Should you wish to stay young and to fascinate your husband — or someone else's husband — a valuable nostrum is prescribed. Do you have disagreeable warts? He will take them off you. Have you not heard of Dr. Anselm's Balsamic Cordial for Ladies in Nature's Decay?"

"A charlatan?"

"God, who in the physical profession is not? They all have their cure-alls. But his, I believe, are more effective than most."

"A pity he cannot prescribe to make himself a thought prettier. Why do you say I should not look at the scenery?"

"Well, not to *admire* it. Some of these poets nowadays, my dear, offend me to distraction. They have a *romantic* view of life. It is so low-class, so mediocre. What are mountains and lakes, to be stared at as if they were of *interest?* Personally, when I go through the Alps I always draw the blinds of my coach."

"And who is that coming in now?" Elizabeth asked. "Like Dr. Anselm somewhat, but smaller."

"That, my dear, is another man of some import in the world, though no doubt as a high Tory you must disapprove of him — as I do. I could spit him on a sword for his wrong assumptions about the war. The Hon. Charles James Fox. And that's his wife, the former Mrs.

Armistead, whom he married a mere four years ago.''

The big Dr. Anselm waddled past. He had eyebrows like black slugs, mottled black hair which he did not deign to cover with a wig, and a stomach which spread from his chest and preceded him as he walked. Mr. and Mrs. Fox turned the other way.

''Ah,'' said Monk, ''this one, this tall feller, is Lord Walsingham, who's chairman of the committees in the House of Lords. And behind him, the younger one, is George Canning, who's secretary for foreign affairs. I'm glad to see a few of the government turning up, else we should be swamped with the dissidents. Instruct me, where does George get his shoes?''

''My George? I don't know.''

''Well, it is not the right place. Tell him to go to Rymer's. Outstanding, my dear. And Wagner's for hats. One can never afford to have anything but the best.''

''I'm sure George would entirely agree,'' Elizabeth said with a touch of irony, and, to be polite, spoke to Miss

Page. So the group re-formed.

Ross and Demelza were talking to a Mr. and Mrs. John Bullock. Bullock was the member for Essex, an elderly man and in confirmed opposition to Pitt, but he and Ross liked and respected each other. They were joined by the Baron Duff of Fife and his daughter, who was wearing a startling necklace that seemed to set fire to her throat.

When they had gone Demelza said: "There is so much wealth in London! Did you see that — those diamonds! And yet there's so little."

"Little what?"

"Wealth. Those faces as we came in! They would fight for a sixpence. Sometimes I think — what little I've seen, Ross — it's as if London's half at war with itself."

"Explain yourself, my love."

"Well, isn't it? All the crime. It's like a — a volcano. In the streets — those gangs at corners waiting for a victim. All the drunkenness and the quarrelling. The thieves and the prostitutes and the beggars. The stone throwing. The fighting with clubs. The starvation. And then this. All this luxury. Is this how it was in France?"

"Yes. And worse."

"I see how you must feel sometimes."

"I'm glad you feel it too. But don't let it spoil your evening."

"Oh, no. Oh, no."

He looked at her. "Sometimes I think we have as much control of events as straws in a stream."

A few moments later the Warleggans came into view on the other side of the room.

Demelza said: "Is Elizabeth going to have another child?"

"What?" Ross stared. "How do you know?"

"I don't. It's just a look she has."

"You could very well be right," he said after a moment. "She was indisposed the day of the opening of the hospital. Fortunately for me, she was taken with a fainting fit, or I should have had violent words with George, if not worse, and then I'm sure Francis Basset would not have thought me a suitable partner for his banking concerns."

"Straws in a stream," said Demelza. "How lucky we were!"

On the other side of the room Adderley said to George: "Did you actually *go and listen* to the speech from the throne, my dear?"

"Yes," said George.

"All this nonsense about militia? I could not bear it. I spent my time at Boodles. You're down, you know. The election's in November. I can arrange the necessary support."

"I'm obliged, Monk. I see Poldark's here."

"The noble captain. Yes. You don't like him, do you."

"No."

"You Cornishmen take yourselves so serious. What's in a feud? Who's that with him?"

"His wife. He married his kitchenmaid."

"Well, she's a good looker."

"Some men have thought so."

"With success?"

"Probably," said George, old malice stirring.

Adderley put up his glass to look across the room. "Her hair's provincial. Pity. The rest is good."

"Oh, no doubt she's been dressed in London."

"So she should be *un*dressed in London, don't you think? I cannot bear virtuous countrywomen."

"They are fewer than you think."

"Oh, yes, I know, my dear. Is there in truth one such in the land? Well, you know my claim."

"What's that?"

"I've never turned a woman empty away."

"You should try your luck."

"I'll test the water. Drommie!"

"Yes?" said the girl.

"Come with me. There's a feller I wish you to meet."

III

"This is Adderley coming across to us now," Ross said in an undertone.

"Who is he?"

"Friend of George's. He was down at

Trenwith last summer. A member of Parliament. Ex-captain in a foot regiment, like me. A wild man.''

"Wilder than you?"

"Different."

"With his wife?"

"I doubt it."

Demelza eyed the man as he came towards them, erect, thin as a pole, pale-faced. He was dressed in a dark olive-green spotted silk coat and breeches, the suit embossed with silver.

"My dear Poldark, I didn't see you at the opening today! May I present Miss Drommie Page? Captain Poldark. And *Mrs*. Poldark, I presume? *Enchanté*. I suppose the King didn't actually *read* his speech, did he?"

"No, it was read for him. Were you not there?"

"No, my dear, that's why I didn't see you. How drab it is to be recalled to London so early merely to pass some flatulent bill to do with the militia. The stinks haven't subsided yet. Do you live distant, Mrs. Poldark?"

"In Cornwall."

"But of course. Your husband not only sits in the Boscawen interest but *lives* there! Greater love hath no man!"

They talked for a few minutes, Adderley's snake-grey eyes travelling assessingly over Demelza's face and figure, Demelza smiling up at him from time to time and then glancing away, taking in the colour and the lights and the strolling, chatting figures and the palm trees and the music from a further room.

"Rot me," said Monk, dabbing his nose with a lace handkerchief, "I'm as hungry as a cannibal. Shall we go in to supper, Mistress Poldark?"

"Rot me too," said Demelza, and took a further look around the room.

"Well, then?"

"I'm sorry, sir, but I am engaged."

"By whom?"

"My husband."

"Your husband! My dear, it is simply not done! It is not permitted for married people to eat together! Not in London society."

"I'm sorry. I thought it was . . . But

if you feel like a cannibal, might you not mistake what you were eating?"

Adderley's eyes crinkled. "That I might, ma'am. You, for instance. I have a catholic taste. Look . . . Poldark is busy with Drommie. He can lead her in. I promise we'll sit at the same table."

Swift thoughts: this man George's friend: Ross doesn't like him: but this an evening out: how to refuse? . . . needless offence . . .

She said: "Then let us all go in together! Ross . . . Captain Adderley is becoming ferocious for food. Shall we all eat now?"

She saw a mild glint on Ross's face when he turned, though it would have been imperceptible to anyone less attuned to his feelings.

He said: "By all means," though the words lacked enthusiasm.

On Adderley's arm Demelza walked to the supper room, followed by Ross and Andromeda.

"So you find me ferocious," Monk said. "I would not have thought you a woman easily intimidated,

Mistress Poldark."

"Ah, very easily, Captain Adderley."

"Is it my reputation that frightens you?"

"I don't know your reputation, sir."

"Two things I like best of all: to fight and to make love."

"With the same person?"

"No, but on the same day. One whets the appetite for the other, ma'am."

In the next room a great table was heavy with food prepared in the most extravagant and artistic fashion. According to your tastes a white-hatted servant behind the table would cut you a piece of Windsor Castle, Buckingham House, St. Paul's, Westminster Abbey; or a whale, a giant dormouse, a horse, or a crocodile. Since they were early on the scene most of these wonders were unscathed, and everyone who entered the room gasped at the artistic ingenuity they must help to ruin.

"It looks," said George, "as if we have lost our friends."

"Yes," Elizabeth said; "I am somewhat surprised at Monk's taste."

"Oh, I set him after them. There's nothing Monk rises to so quickly as a challenge."

"I didn't mean the Poldarks," Elizabeth replied a little acidly. "I meant the young lady he had chosen to bring with him."

"Oh, Miss Page. They say she's the natural daughter of Lord Keppel. Pretty but penniless and vicious: it's a common tale. Oh, your lordship . . ."

"Sir?"

"Warleggan. You remember, at Ranelagh? May I introduce you to my wife. Viscount Calthorp; Elizabeth."

In the outer hall nearly all the guests had arrived. The Prince of Wales had sent a late message regretting that he would be unable to be present.

"Well," said Caroline to her husband, "the worst is nearly over. I trust you're not wishing yourself back with your patients."

"No," said Dwight, smiling. In fact he had that moment been reflecting that Mrs. Coad, in extremis when he last called, would be dead before the end of the month. And Char Nanfan struck with an inexplicable sickness. And Ed Bartle's children, three down with a pulmonary infection following the scarlet fever . . .

"Come, let us go and eat," Caroline said, linking her arm in his. "Some of the tabbies up here have been doubting that I really *have* a husband. I must display you all I can!"

"Where are Ross and Demelza?"

"I don't know. I saw them just now . . . Oh, with Monk Adderley and his pretty piece! That *is* a surprise. Well, then, we must eat with someone else."

"I imagine they must have been invited, for I don't believe they would ever have chosen that company," said Dwight. "Was that Lord Falmouth who came in just now? With the old lady?"

"Yes. His mother. We're honoured, since he is very little more sociable in London than in Cornwall."

They moved back into the reception room, where servants were discreetly rearranging the chairs so that later in the evening there would be room to dance.

Monk Adderley had steered Demelza into a corner seat while Ross and the girl were still choosing their food.

"Those are handsome buttons," Demelza said, pointing to the large ones he wore on each sleeve.

"Yes? You notice the lock of hair preserved in each?"

"That's what I thought it was. How nicely worked. Do they — does the hair belong to Miss Page?"

"No, to a Lieutenant Framfield. He was the last man I killed."

For the first time Demelza noticed the scar on the side of his head, half hidden by his stiff, curled hair.

"The last?"

"Well, two is all. And another maimed."

"Do you not get put in prison for murder? On even hanged?"

"Fair fight is not murder. Of course there is sometimes a trial. The first time I pleaded benefit of clergy."

"Are you a clergyman?"

Adderley's eyes crinkled again. It seemed to be the nearest he ever came to laughing. "A cleric, my dear. A clerk. I can write. I was excused on those grounds and sentenced only to be branded."

"Branded?"

"Yes . . . with a cold iron. Let me show you the mark." He extended his long thin hand in which the bones and veins delicately showed. She repressed a shiver.

"There is no mark . . . Oh, I *see.*"

"The second time I was found guilty of manslaughter and sentenced to ten days in prison."

"And the third time you really *will* be hanged?" she asked politely.

"Who knows? Who cares? Ah, here's Poldark with my little girl. I feel sorry for Drommie."

"Why sorry? Ross is good company — if he likes his company."

"Which he appears not altogether to be doing at this moment. No, my dear, I meant on other counts. Drommie has a beautiful body. I should know. I have investigated it thoroughly. I could commend her to any sculptor. But as to her mind, I do not think there will ever be anything more important in it than a hairpin."

The lady being so discussed said to Ross: "Are you *strong?* You look *very* strong." Her voice and eyes were full of a bored innuendo.

"Very," he said, looking her over.

"How interesting." She yawned. "How vastly interesting."

"But I'd warn you. I have one weak leg."

She looked down. "Which one?"

"They take it in turns."

After an appreciable moment she tapped him on the shoulder with her fan. "Captain Poldark, you're making merry with me."

"I wouldn't presume on such short acquaintance. Has Captain Adderley never told you the old infantryman's adage?"

"What is that?"

"It's one leg of an elephant saying to another: 'Damn your eyes, move a little quicker.' "

"I call that quaint." She yawned again.

"Is it past your bedtime, Miss Page?"

"No . . . I've only just got up."

"My daughter's just like that."

"How old is she?"

"Nearly five."

"Now you're jesting again."

"I swear it's the truth."

"*No* . . . I mean by comparing *me!* Is Monk a friend of yours?"

"It would seem so."

"And of your wife's?"

"That remains to be seen."

"Of course. She's vastly attractive."

"I think so."

"And me?"

He looked at her. "You?"

"Yes . . . what do you think of me?"

He considered. "I think it *is* past your bedtime."

"That could be considered an insult, Captain Poldark."

"Oh, *no!*"

"Or — as a compliment . . ."

He smiled at her. "Oh, yes," he said.

People sat at tables of varying size, and wine and bread and knives and forks were rapidly put before them. Adderley had chosen a table for four, which made them somewhat isolated from the rest. Ross bore the company he did not want with great good humour, and only occasionally rose to bait that was put before him. As when Adderley began to speak of the expenses of the last election and how it had cost Lord Mandeville and Thomas Fellowes upwards of £13,000 between them to get in, of which he'd been told, by God, that nearly £7,000 had gone in innkeepers' bills. And how lucky he and Ross were to be the tame lapdogs of an indulgent peer.

"I think our 'indulgent peer' is here tonight," Demelza put in as she saw Ross about to speak. "I haven't seen him for upwards of two years, Ross, and I must ask him how Mrs. Gower is."

And, said Adderley, how old Reynolds was known in the House as the Dinner Gong, because whenever he got up to speak a hundred and forty members would walk out. And how on one occasion two years ago, a distinguished lady sitting in the strangers' gallery, caught up in a long debate, had been unable to contain herself, so that what she spilled fell upon the head of old John Luttrell, thereby ruining both his hat and his coat. "And twas lucky it did not blind him, by God!" said Adderley.

Miss Page went off into little muffled screeches of laughter. "How deliciously vulgar of you, Monk! I call that entertaining!"

"Don't tell me," said Monk to the others, "that you do not appreciate the anecdote! Walpole always encouraged vulgar conversation on the grounds that it was the only talk all could enjoy."

"Not at all," said Ross. "For are we not all vulgars ourselves?"

No one spoke for a moment.

"In what way?"

"Of a common or usual kind. You cannot suppose there is a uniqueness in human beings that puts one or an other above the rest — *surely!* Common, customary, or familiar. We all share the same hungers and the same functions: the young and the old, the lord and the beggar. Only the perverse fail to laugh and cry at the same things. That's common sense. Vulgar common sense."

The uneasy supper went on to its end,

and presently broke up, and the ladies retired and the men also, and when they came down dancing had begun; and an hour passed pleasantly. Monk danced once with Demelza, and then not again, for Dwight took her away, and then Ross, and then other men intervened. She was not sure of the most fashionable steps, but what she knew seemed to suffice.

It was not until there was a brief interval at one o'clock that Monk, noticing her briefly alone, came across to her.

"When may I see you again, Mrs. Poldark?"

"But you are seeing me now, Captain Adderley."

"Is this your very first visit to London?"

"You know it is."

"Well, if I may say so, ma'am, I see you as a person of great undeveloped potentiality. My dear, you've scarce lived yet, believe me!"

"I've lived very well, thank you, Captain Adderley."

"You have not tasted the sophisticated pleasures."

"I always think they are only for folk who have tired of the simple ones."

"I'll wait upon you. When will your husband be out?"

"When I am." ·

"Then I'll wait upon you when he is in."

"You're most kind."

"I hope you will be also." His eyes went up along the lines of her peach-coloured gown, noting where it clung, to her bare arms and shoulders and low neck, the pale olive swelling of her breasts; at last up to her face and eyes, and his expression conveyed exactly what he would like to do to her. She found herself flushing, an unusual occurrence for her at any time.

Then she felt a hand put into her gloved hand. It was Ross, come up behind her.

"Adderley, you must return to your Miss Page. She is greatly lacking your attentions."

"Do you know, Poldark," Monk said gently, "there is only one person I ever take instructions from, and that is myself."

Demelza squeezed Ross's hand to stop his reply.

"Ross," she said, "Captain Adderley has paid us the compliment of saying he would wait upon us. While that would be — quite delightful, I was suggesting instead that we should all meet at the play on Thursday. You were telling me that we should go, Captain Adderley."

She could sense the hesitation on both sides. Since Adderley had told her nothing of the sort, it represented to him a small deception of her husband and therefore progress along the road he wished to pursue. Ross had indeed talked of going to the play, and a blank refusal at this point could only have been seen as an affront.

Adderley said: "That would be amusing, my dear. The play I have seen twice and it's tedious. But the women are interesting."

And so it was settled.

CHAPTER IV

By three in the morning people were beginning to depart. Caroline had seen what had been happening to Demelza, and took Monk Adderley off on her own and away from the danger zone.

Later she said to Demelza: "Sometimes I think him a little crazed. *Not* because he has taken a fancy to you! But because he is at times so . . . ungoverned in his behaviour. Treat it lightly — as a joke."

"That's all very well, but — "

"I know. But *explain* to Ross . . . I'll suggest to Dwight that we also go on Thursday. And in the meantime I will see what else there is in the pool of young women who might be dandled in front of Monk's nose to divert him."

. . . As they were waiting for their carriages to draw up George said:

"So you burned your fingers, Monk."

"Not at all, my dear. *Rome n'a été bâti tout en un jour.* One has to make the preliminary — clearances."

"And you have made those? I don't believe it! She is a virtuous woman!"

"You told me not."

"Well, who knows about any one of us? I said she was probably not. Perhaps later you will be able to inform me for sure."

"Of course. I can inform you now. Within a month she will not be a virtuous woman — if by virtue you mean faithfulness to her husband. I shall consider her virtuous if she is faithful to me, for as long as I want her."

"It's a big claim. I would be tempted to wager on it."

"My dear, by all means. Nothing would give me greater satisfaction. What odds will you offer?"

George licked his lips, and glanced across to see that Elizabeth was not within hearing. "A hundred guineas to ten. I am not prepared to make longer odds than that, for, after all, if you win you get all the fun."

"No," said Monk, looking at his friend with his cold eyes. "I perceive that if I win you will be more satisfied than I."

The Poldark coach was called soon after, and Demelza was handed in, and they moved creakingly away. There was silence for a while and then Ross said:

"Monk Adderley is a freakish fellow."

"Freakish . . . yes. I am a little scared at him."

"It did not seem so. You asked him to join us at supper and have invited him to the theatre on Thursday."

Demelza struggled with the difficulty of explaining. "In the first instance he had just asked me to go into supper with him *alone*. I'm not sure of the courtesies in London, but I thought it might be insulting to refuse. So I suggested we should all go together."

"And in the second instance?"

"I thought he and you were going to start growling at each other like a couple of tomcats, so I said the first thing that came into my head to stop it."

They were crossing Oxford Road, and

even at this late hour there were people about, drunks lying in the shelter of overhanging houses, drays and butchers' carts rattling over the cobbles on late or early errands, beggars picking over the refuse and the droppings.

Ross said: "It's strange that people who affect to find life endlessly tedious are themselves so tedious to know. Well, I suppose we must endure him on Thursday."

"Ross." Demelza turned her head and the light from a passing link boy showed up her intent expression. "Caroline had a word with me about him during the evening. She told us not to take him serious. Not me. Not you. Especially not you. She said you must always treat him as a joke."

Ross pursed his lips. "Adderley. Yes. He is a joke. But I think we must watch him lest the joke turn sour."

II

They took a box at Drury Lane, which cost Ross twenty shillings and held four seats, and there saw Mr. John Kemble, Mr. William Barrymore, and Mrs. Powell in *The Revenge,* a tragedy in five acts by Edward Young. Demelza had not seen a play since the one performed in their library more than ten years ago, and that was a mere charade compared to this. She forgot the pale man, taut as a wire, in the chair beside her, who took what opportunities he could to put his face against hers to whisper comments and to touch her bare forearm with his thin cool fingers. She was far more annoyed by the noise from the pit; the scrambles that took place, the flying oranges, the shouts at the actors if something was displeasing. The light from the three hundred flickering tallow candles was so disposed behind the scenes that the stage was clearly but subtly lit. The brilliance of the costumes and the scenery, the resonance and drama of the actors' voices, all cast a spell on her. Between the acts there was music to keep the audience entertained, and when *The Revenge* was over in a welter of blood and tragedy, two more short pieces were staged, as comic as the main piece had been sad. A wonderful evening.

Dwight and Caroline were in the next box, and in one interval Dwight was able to say to Ross:

"I met Dr. Jenner today."

Ross looked vague. He had been more than a little preoccupied with angers that were swirling up in him and then dispersing in waves of self-mockery.

"Jenner? Oh? This book you were reading . . ."

"I believe it may be one of the great discoveries of our time. Of course there have been inoculations against the smallpox for some years, but this is different. There has not yet, in my view, been sufficient experiment. But I am hoping to see him again before I leave."

"You are off home?"

Dwight smiled. "Not yet."

Half joking, Ross said: "Perhaps I shall have to take Demelza home soon. She is not going to be safe here."

"I believe she's safe, Ross. She can look to herself."

"That," said Ross, "was what I used to think."

The last short play was nothing but a musical lampoon, a satire on the new fashions, all of them grossly exaggerated on the stage. The song that caught the public fancy was sung by a Miss Fanny Thompson and went:

Shepherd, I have lost my waist,
Have you seen my body?
Sacrificed to modern taste,
I'm quite a Hoddy-Doddy.
Tis gone, and I have not the nook
For cheese cake, tart or jelly.
For fashion I that part forsook
Where sages place the belly!

Everyone joined in the second and third choruses. It became a great roar of sound.

As the two thousand people were streaming out of the theatre Monk Adderley said: "Will you visit Vauxhall with me on Monday next, Mrs. Poldark? I believe there is likely to be a late sitting of the house."

"Should you not be present, then?"

"God forbid. But your husband will."

"Tell me," she said. "Why did they call you Monk? It seems — not apt."

The eyes crinkled again. In a less sinister face it would have been attractive. "Not apt, as you observe, my dear. My father was so called and so liked his name that he has given it to all my brothers, to make sure it should be perpetuated."

She raised her eyebrows. "Dear life! Do you mean there are several more Monk Adderleys walking the streets of London?"

"No, ma'am. Two died in infancy. One had his throat cut in India. One is in Bristol still with my parents, but he is a tedious provincial boy who will grow up into a country squire. . . . But tell me of *your* name. What does it mean in that bizarre Celtic language you have?"

"I don't know," said Demelza, knowing well, but feeling it was a bad thing to give him a further lead.

"Well, it is a passably provoking name. Ecod it is . . . Demelza . . . Demelza . . .

It needs to be peeled off — like a cloak, like clothes, like a skin . . ."

"Like a banana?" she suggested.

"Listen, satin arms," he said, "I will take so much from you and no more. You have a sharp tongue, which I shall find very entertaining in due course. And shall know what to do with. On Monday, then. At nine."

Before Demelza could speak Caroline said: "There's room for two in our coach. We'll take you home. Can you find a chair, Monk?"

Adderley said: "I shall go to White's for an hour. Would you care to accompany me, Poldark? You can go in as my guest."

Ross hesitated, and then said amiably: "Thank you, no, I think not. I'm not rich enough to be able to lose money nor poor enough to wish to gain it."

"What a tedious thought," said Adderley. "The importance of money is that it should be treated as of no importance."

III

Later that night, just as Demelza was dozing off to sleep, Ross said:

"D'you know for once I believe Adderley was right."

"What? What about? What d'you mean?"

"That money should always be looked on as unimportant. Now that I run a tin mine and have interests in rolling mills and the rest I am becoming too attached to the stuff."

"I have never been *un*attached to the stuff," she said. "Maybe it's because I was born a miner's daughter. Maybe it's because I've never had so very much. All I know is that having coins in my purse makes me happy, and having no coins makes me sad. I can't work it out different."

"All the same," Ross said, "Adderley may be right in that, but he is wrong in all else. Wrong especially if he supposes I shall stand by and watch him attempting to cuckold me."

"And do you serious think he has the

slightest chance?"

Ross did not answer.

Demelza sat sharply up in bed, wide awake now.

"Ross, what are you *thinking* of? You are not serious in supposing . . . Because *once* something happened, because once I felt deeply about another man; do you think, do you suppose I am like to do that again — with the first such who comes along? Am I condemned — because of — of Hugh Armitage — to be suspected of feeling the same for every man who pays me some special attention?" When he still didn't speak she said: *"Ross!"*

"No," he said judicially.

"It could not happen again — certainly not with a man like Captain Adderley."

"Then you should make it clearer to me that it can't."

"How?"

"By not encouraging him."

"I do *not* encourage him! I have to be polite!"

"Why?"

She made a despairing gesture. "Sometimes, Ross, you try me hard.

You really do. I am — I am in London for the first time. It is a new society. I am your wife — truly, truly in more than name again, in more than mere *act* again, after so long. I am *happy,* excited, living in a new way. A man comes up to me and starts paying me compliments. He is a — he is educated, well-bred, a member of Parliament. Do I turn my back on him to please you? Do I smack his face to satisfy you? Do I sit in a corner and refuse to answer him? Better that I should never have come!"

"Better that you should never have come than that he should contrive to paw you. He must know every bone in your left arm from wrist to shoulder."

There was silence.

"Then tell me what I must do," Demelza said. "Do you wish me to go home?"

"Of course not!"

"Tell me how I must behave then."

"You know very well how to behave."

"That's not fair! Anyway," Demelza said mutinously, "he won't take no for an answer. He says he is coming to take me to Vauxhall next Monday when you are in the House."

"And shall you go?"

"Certainly not! I shall be out — or unwell. A fever might be most likely to cool his ardour . . . Perhaps I could paint some spots on my face and squint through the window at him . . . Ross, do not let this spoil our time here . . ."

"No," he said, "no," and put an arm about her shoulder, "but one cannot always contain or order one's feelings, and when I see you in the company of another man — being touched and pressed by him — my mind — or something in me — turns up old feelings, old thoughts, old resentments. Which aren't so very old."

She lay against him, saying nothing for a long time, but not so sleepy now.

IV

A basket of flowers came next morning. Ross was for throwing it out, but Demelza could not tolerate this. Flowers to her were objects of interest and pleasure, no matter where they came from; and there were some in this bunch that she had never seen before.

They spent the Sunday with Dwight and Caroline riding beyond the village of Hampstead, and dined and supped with them. On the Monday morning more flowers. On Monday at five-thirty Caroline came for her and they went to the other royal theatre, in the Covent Garden. It was over at nine and Demelza, feeling she was eating too much, declined an invitation to go back to Hatton Garden to sup and said she would eat lightly at home. Caroline left her there and she went up, to see lights in their sitting room. She burst in, supposing that Ross was back, and found Monk Adderley reclining in a chair.

He was in an eggshell-blue suit of the finest silk, and his shirt was ornate with amber buttons.

"Oh, welcome," he said, getting up slowly. "You have kept me waiting, but no matter. The pleasure is the greater."

"How did you get in?"

"By the front door and up the stairs, ma'am. It was not difficult." He bowed over her hand, and she saw the scar in his hair.

"Did — Mrs. Parkins let you in?"

"Yes. I said I was your brother. A simple device." He peeled back her glove and put his lips to the back of her wrist. "I always believe in simplicity first. Mind, there was an occasion last year when I wanted to enter a young lady's apartment, and an old dragon of a mother was downstairs and inspected everyone who went up. So I borrowed the clothes of a seamstress and the old dragon passed me without a second glance! I make a tolerably good girl."

"I'm sorry," Demelza said, "I must ask you to leave, Captain Adderley."

"*Leave?* Do I offend you? How prettily you have arranged my flowers!"

"It was kind of you to send them to me." She knelt and poked at the fire, put on two pieces of coal, giving herself time to think. "But it does not entitle you to — to . . ."

"To enter your apartments by a stratagem? Oh, come. I had no other way of discovering you alone."

"Why do you wish to?"

"Look in the glass, my dear."

"I — am married, Captain Adderley."

"Oh, yes. That I do know." A hint of amusement in his voice.

"And my husband would not like to find you here."

"Nor shall he. I have a man outside who will delay him long enough in the street to enable me to slip away by the back entrance. But that is unlikely to be for two hours yet. They are droning on about the militia."

"Please go. I don't wish to send for Mrs. Parkins."

"I would not wish you to. But can we not at least talk a little while?"

"What about?"

"Any subject under the sun you choose. Life. Love. Letters. Let me tell you of the men I've killed."

"Next time we meet."

He went across to a vase. "Look at these. Do you see these? Do you know what these flowers are called?"

"No."

"They are called dahlias. D-a-h-l-i-a-s.

They have been imported into England for use by the poor in place of the potato. But the saucy poor do not like the flavour; so now they are selling not the root but the flower.''

He had come up to her again as he was speaking but she moved away.

''You will notice that they have no scent.''

''I've noticed that.''

''Let me relieve you of your cloak.''

''When you have gone,'' she said.

His eyes were very narrow. ''Are you afraid of me?''

''Not a bit.''

''Do you dislike me?''

''No-o.''

''You sound a little uncertain. Are you afraid of what I might do to you? Have you never had a man but your husband? Don't you want to understand any of the finer complexities of love?''

''Are you talking about love at all, Captain Adderley?''

He shrugged. ''Call it what you will. I can instruct you most delicately in it all.''

There was a moment's pause. He put his fingers gently on her breast; they lay there as light as a paw; then she as quietly moved away again.

He said: "You see?"

She turned: "What do I see?"

"How quickly you respond."

"You flatter yourself."

"Do I? Let me prove it."

She shook her head.

"I am — deeply enamoured," he said. "Don't suppose this is some trivial fancy. You are a very enchanting woman."

"I am — deeply flattered," she said. "But — "

"Let us sit down and I will tell you of your enchantment."

"I'm sorry."

"Why are you so harsh?"

"Harsh? Not at all! I just happen not to feel as you wish me to feel."

"It could be altered, I assure you. I have a sovereign remedy, which I will explain to you — "

"Not now. Another time, sir."

They stared at each other.

He said: "You have a strange voice,

ecod. It's West Country, I suppose."

"I come from the West Country."

"Well, I like it. Do you cry out when a man takes you?"

She drew a deep breath. "In a moment — in a moment I think you will call me a prude, so perhaps I should say it now to save you the bother — "

"Ma'am, you put words into my mouth that I — "

"Are you a gentleman?"

He flushed. "I trust so." It was the first time she had ever seen colour in his face.

"Then — forgive me, as you rightly say I am from the far west and don't understand London manners — but is it not a gentleman's duty to withdraw when a lady ask him?"

His eyes crinkled. "Only when the gentleman has already been in."

That settled it. She went to the bell rope. "I find that — remark a little . . . offensive. Will you please go."

He considered her a moment more, weighing up the probabilities. He took out his handkerchief and dabbed each nostril in turn.

"Perhaps I may wait upon you some other time."

"Please do."

He gave a little sniggering laugh. "Ecod!" he said. "I know what it is. It is not me you're terrified of, it's your husband! Does he beat you?"

"Yes, often."

"When his arm gets tired," Monk Adderley said, "tell him to send for me. Good night, Mrs. Poldark."

V

The Poldarks' second week was not as pleasant as the first. Demelza had told Ross of Adderley's visit, though she had glossed over the details. It was better that he should know from her than find out by accident and suppose she was deceiving him. He reprimanded Mrs. Parkins: in future no one must be admitted to their rooms while they were out, whatever the pretext. But their relationship did not settle down to what it had been before. A cloud of non-explanation and misunderstanding lay around them and could give rise to forked lightning at any time.

They visited the Royal Academy and the British Museum, and at the beginning of the third week they supped with the Boscawens at their house in Audley Street. This was not as much of an ordeal as Demelza had feared, since the Viscount's mother, the widow of the great admiral, was a vivacious old lady and made up for the absence of Mrs. Gower.

When the ladies retired the two men discussed the invasion of Holland, which, after the first successes, was becoming bogged down with problems of supply and by generals and admirals hesitant to take further risks. Lord Falmouth observed dryly that he had heard Captain Poldark had become something of a banker, and Ross explained what had occurred.

"I trust you don't feel this conflicts in any way with my obligation to you as a member of Parliament."

"No . . . Nor would I suppose you would take much heed of me if I said it did."

"There you do me an injustice, my Lord. I would take heed of anything you say. Though obviously . . ."

"Yes, quite."

"But I hope that nowadays there are fewer areas of disagreement between yourself and Lord de Dunstanville . . ."

Lord Falmouth sniffed. "Basset's a pusher, and always has been. He's too *active* about the county. In some cases worthily enough, but most often serving his own ends. However, I believe his peerage has somewhat quieted him down. . . . Now I gather it is *Hawkins* who is befriending the Warleggans. If I know Sir Christopher, it will have been at a price."

"And George Warleggan would be willing to pay it."

"It is interesting," said Falmouth, dusting away the snuff, "if all you say about the Warleggans is true, they have, by putting such pressure on Pascoe's Bank, only succeeded in establishing Pascoe in a stronger position and made the other object of their feud — yourself — into his partner!"

Ross said: "I think Harris Pascoe would greatly prefer his own bank to this new arrangement, but it is true their success was limited. As for me, I don't look on mine as a serious appointment — but, yes, it is diverting, the way it has occurred."

"I would support it," said Lord Falmouth, "were there no other reason than that."

The following Monday there was to be a debate in the House on the new Treaty of Alliance with Russia. It was not something Ross felt deeply involved in, but some of the most famous speakers were likely to take part; Lord Holland was to move an amendment, and Pitt and Fox were likely to take part. So he went at three to get a good seat for the debate, which would open at four.

But in the ordinary course of business of the House, a few smaller bills were in process of debate or amendment beforehand, and in one of these, relating to the treatment and succour of disabled soldiers and sailors, there was a call for a division, instead of for the customary show of hands, and Ross was sufficiently concerned to vote for the bill.

When such a division took place only one side was called to go out; and they were then counted as they came in again. The other side remained in their seats. It was the Speaker's responsibility to nominate which side should have to go, but normally he chose the side proposing and supporting a new bill. So it was in this case, and perhaps Ross should have known better than to move.

In a house which would barely seat 300 when the total numbers were 558 there was likely to be pressure for seats before an important debate; and it was the custom of the House that any member who vacated his seat to vote was liable to forfeit it. For this reason members often failed to vote for a bill they supported so that they should not lose their seats, and sometimes it was a tactic to call for a division, knowing that fewer people would walk out to support than would have called "Aye!"

In this case the bill was carried on its first reading by a majority of thirteen but when Ross returned he found his seat occupied by Captain Monk Adderley.

"Ah . . ." said Ross.

Adderley looked up at him through half-closed lids.

"Lost something, Poldark?"

"Yes . . . my seat."

"That you cannot have, my dear. There is no such thing as *my* seat in this house, as you well know. You'll have to go and stand at the back, won't you."

A fat little man next to Monk chuckled but kept his eyes down.

"Is there such a thing as *my* gloves?" Ross asked.

"*Your* gloves? You should know, Poldark. Why should I?"

"Because I left them in this place. It occurred to me you might be sitting on them."

"I?" said Adderley, and yawned. "Not at all, my dear. I would not touch them. You see, I'm no longer interested in any of your . . . your worn possessions."

So many people were still walking about — others returning were trying to squeeze into seats — a man was on his feet speaking, or trying to speak, on some other bill — that only a dozen witnessed the sharp movement — scuffle — that broke out on the back benches. Ross's hand had flown out and clutched Adderley by the cravat; Adderley was hauled to his feet; with his other hand Ross picked up his gloves; Adderley was dropped back with a thump.

"Order! Order!" some members shouted.

"I beg your pardon, Adderley," Ross said, and handed him his hat, which had fallen off. "I felt sure my gloves were here. I beg your pardon, sir," he said, bowing to the Speaker, and left the Chamber.

VI

About two hours later a Mr. John Craven arrived at George Street and delivered a letter. It said:

Dear Poldark,
The Insult you paid me in the House was of a nature that brooks no apology. I know you to be an

infamous braggart, and believe all your display of courage to be the mask for a cowardly disposition. I therefore desire to give you the opportunity of showing me whether this epithet is rightly applied or not.

I desire that you meet me in Hyde Park on Wednesday at 6 A.M. with a brace of pistols each, to determine our differences. My second, Mr. John Craven, carries this letter and I desire you to tell him whom you will appoint to represent you.

I desire that this Meeting be kept a dead secret, for reasons which must be plain to you.

I am, Sir, your humble servant,

Monk Adderley

CHAPTER V

Demelza was out when the letter came. He
said nothing to her when she came back.
That evening he walked round and had a
talk with Dwight.

Dwight said: "But this is monstrous! A
brief scuffle in the House? They're always
happening! The man's *mad!* That injury
to his head. I should ignore the whole
thing."

"I have already written accepting."

Dwight stared at Ross as if unable to
believe what he heard. "You have
what? . . ."

"I have accepted."

"But, Ross! You should *not* have done!
The whole thing must be stopped at
once!"

"It can't be."

"But — but there's nothing at *stake!*

The merest storm in a teacup . . . In any event, the fellow's a noted duellist. He's killed two or three men!''

''So have I.''

''In duels?''

''Well, no. But I'm accustomed to using a gun. As the rooks know when they raid my crops.''

''That's not a pistol, Ross! How long since you used one of those?''

''I'll take some practice tomorrow. You know why I came here? To ask you to be my second. Indeed, presuming on our friendship, I've already given your name.''

Dwight bit at his glove. They were pacing the street outside Caroline's house, and it was beginning to rain.

''Well?'' said Ross.

''Yes, I'll be your second,'' Dwight said abruptly, ''because then I have the right to interfere and see what may be done to have the whole scandalous nonsense called off.''

''Small chance of that. Also — it is of advantage that you should be there, because in the event of either of us being wounded we shall need to look no further for a surgeon."

Dwight frowned at the letter by the yellow light of one of the street lamps. "What is the meaning of this emphasis on secrecy? I know of course — "

"John Craven explained it. If Adderley should be — accurate with his ball it is essential that it should not be known that he is responsible. If he stood a *third* trial he would be likely to go to prison for some years."

"As he deserves anyhow. But good God, he is the *challenger!* Are we to accept *his* conditions? I never heard of anything more outrageous!"

"It will suit me well," Ross said. "If I should kill Adderley it will not suit me to stand a trial either. Once is enough."

Dwight looked at his friend's dark face. "It will get about. This sort of thing can never be altogether hushed up."

"Well, that is something we shall both have to risk."

They stopped where a cellar trapdoor was open and two men like black dwarfs were unloading casks of ale from a dray. Beside it someone had tipped a load of bricks, making passage along the uneven pavement impossible.

"Does Demelza know aught of this?"

"No, and must not! Nor Caroline. Fortunately there is only a day to wait. Remember this, Dwight; you are sworn to secrecy. *No one* must be told."

"And are you proposing that we should go to Strawberry Hill tomorrow as arranged?"

"Of course. Otherwise they will guess something is in the wind."

Dwight shook his head in despair.

"And when will you get your pistol practice?"

"First thing. We don't leave until ten."

"So I must also be about early on my efforts at a reconciliation. Ross, what are the grounds on which you would agree to withdraw?"

"I have nothing to withdraw, Dwight. I have only accepted the challenge."

Dwight gestured irritably. "To say that you meant no offence in the House?"

"I apologised to him at the time."

"Did he hear it?"

"He should have done."

"Did you mean it?"

"No."

They turned back, towards the top of the Garden and the better houses.

"So . . . I never thought when I came to London that I should be involved in such a childish, *wicked* affair as this. Because it is *both,* Ross. When there is so much suffering and pain in the world already . . . And when we are at war. There is enough killing to be done without fighting among ourselves."

"You must tell Adderley that. If he wishes to withdraw his challenge on those grounds — or on any other honourable grounds — I'll be willing to let the matter drop."

Dwight said: "You speak as if you would not *really* be willing."

After a moment Ross said: "You know me too well, Dwight. Anyway, I leave it in your hands."

At ten next morning the quartet set out for Strawberry Hill. The house, built by the great Sir Horace Walpole, was one of the sights Caroline had planned they should see. It was fine again, after the cold rain of yesterday, with balustrades of white cloud arranging themselves in the west; a good day to clear the smells of London; a good day for riding; and the distance little more than ten miles.

In a few minutes alone before they left Dwight was able to gesture his disgust and say: "If it were possible, he is more intransigeant than you. But while perhaps he has some excuse, being unstable, you have none."

"What would you have me do?" Ross asked. "Go to his lodgings and knock on his door and when he comes kneel and offer him an abject apology? An apology that I became annoyed at his insult to my wife?"

"Are you sure it was intended as such?"

"Of course. Nothing else."

"In any event a challenge like this is not important coming from such as him. I would suggest you go to see him this evening and tell him you have no interest in his false heroics. You are a veteran of the American war. If he calls you a coward people will only laugh — at him."

Ross smiled but did not reply.

They reached Twickenham at midday. Walpole had now been dead a couple of years, but the Hon. Mrs. Damer, the daughter of Walpole's great friend General Conway, was in residence and was maintaining the tradition of allowing only four people to visit the house daily.

Demelza found the gardens inspiring. Flowers she had never seen, trees and shrubs she had not imagined. "And, Ross, if we could have a *lawn* like this — or just a little like this — at Nampara. It is so smooth, so *green*." More indulgent towards her than he had been of late, Ross explained that grass would never grow so lush in the sandy soil of the north coast, and that this was all scythed to an inch in height by apprentices learning to be gardeners. Well, Demelza said, when she got home she would do *something*. She could have a lawn of a *sort,* not just tufts of grass pitted with rabbit scratchings and Garrick diggings. Think how much better her hollyhocks would look if you saw them across an expanse of neat, tidy, green lawn! And she saw a shrub like the one Hugh Armitage had given her, and it was called a magnolia. As soon as she saw the name she remembered it.

There was much of interest, too, in the eccentric house with its differing styles; and inside it was a treasure trove: one complete room full of Italian cameos, another with snuffboxes and miniatures. There were water colours and oil paintings and rosaries and bronzes and French glass and Brussels lace and porcelain figures from Dresden and Chinese masks and Turkish swords, and ivory figurines, and fans and clocks, and in a library so many books that it was impossible to guess at the number.

After dinner, on the way home, Demelza suggested that perhaps sometimes it was possible to be *too* rich and so accumulate too much of everything. Nothing, she thought, could be more exciting than to have a passion for something, whether it was fans, or ivory or glass, and then, if you could afford it, to build up a collection, precious piece by precious piece, so that you could put it on your shelves and take pleasure in it every time you saw it. But Sir Horatio, even though he had lived to be old, must have made some of his collections in great *quantities* at the same *time*. How, then, could you find the same pleasure? Six lovely things would always be six lovely things. Six thousand and you'd lose appreciation.

"It's like wives," said Ross. "Enough is enough."

"That cuts both ways," said Caroline. "Though I'm told there is a maharajah in India who lives in his palace, the only man among a thousand women."

"From what I hear," Dwight said, "women were one of the few treasures Walpole did not collect. But I agree with Demelza; a man of the most exquisite taste can still lack taste if he indulges it too freely."

"Like a man of courage?" Ross asked.

"Exactly."

As they drew near London, Caroline said: "Why don't you two sup with us? My aunt always has more on her table than she knows what to do with."

"I had thought," Ross said, "of visiting the theatre again. There is a change of programme. It is a comic play by Goldsmith."

They all looked at him in surprise.

"We'll scarcely be back in time," Caroline said. "We should have no time to change."

"Then go as we are," said Ross. "Or miss the first act. It will be easy to pick up the story."

"Let's go as we are," said Demelza immediately. "What is the hour now? Oh yes, we could do that. And then, perhaps, we could sup afterwards."

So it was agreed. They stabled their horses at an ostler's in Stanhope Street and found seats in a box only five minutes after the curtain had gone up.

Thereafter for two hours they were

brilliantly amused by the play. Sometimes Dwight glanced across at Ross. He knew that neither Ross's nor his own enjoyment could be anything but assumed. It was a remarkable effort of controlled behaviour on Ross's part, and Dwight now and then wondered if the other man, in one of his moods of dark fatalism, had almost totally accepted whatever the future had to bring.

They did not stay for the later plays, but just remained long enough to hear the orchestra in: "Shepherd, I have lost my waist, Have you seen my body? Sacrificed to modern taste, I'm quite a Hoddy-Doddy." Demelza humming it in her slightly husky sweet voice, they were at Hatton Garden by nine o'clock.

Mrs. Pelham was out, so they supped alone. It had just been announced that both houses of Parliament would adjourn early and would not be likely to reassemble before the third week in January; so this set Demelza off — in high spirits after the play — with thoughts of Christmas. Last year had been such a success that she wished exactly to repeat it. Caroline said it was always a mistake to attempt to repeat anything, and anyway Demelza could not, for she, Caroline, intended to spend Christmas in Cornwall this year, and that would break the pattern. Demelza said it would only improve the pattern, whereupon Caroline replied, not at all so, and in fact, although personally she would look on it with some misgiving, she intended to command an attendance at Killewarren of *all* the Poldarks she could muster, not excluding the Blameys, however many of them happened to be not afloat at that particular season. She had heard what a ravishing young man James Blamey was, and she hoped to see for herself. And as for the children, well, she said, Killewarren's bigger than Nampara, so let us hear *some* little feet pattering about it, even if they are not Sarah's.

In a half-wry, half-jolly wrangling supper proceeded, until Mrs. Pelham arrived back with three guests, the first being that tall dark man of forty, the Hon. St. Andrew St. John, who was at present her "special friend." This devoted

684

adherent of Fox was a bachelor, a landowner and a barrister, and had been undersecretary of state for foreign affairs under Fox when only twenty-four. Since then he had been in the wilderness with him; but he enjoyed London social life and most of all, it seemed, Mrs. Pelham. The second was Mr. Edward Coke of Longford, Derbyshire, a man of about the same age, who had made no mark in the House but had much to say out of it, another adherent of Fox; and the third, a rich, sour, sardonic old bachelor called Jeremiah Crutchley, who was member for St. Mawes and had been a friend of Samuel Johnson.

More seats were drawn up round the table, servants scurried with napkins and glasses and wine and dishes of food, and general chatter began. Presently Ross heard St. Andrew St. John mutter something in an undertone to Dwight, and he immediately said:

"May I ask you to repeat that, sir?"

St. John said: "Supper, I think, is a time for *bavarderie,* not serious talk. But I mentioned to your friend that it is reported General Buonaparte has given the blockading squadrons the slip and reached France.''

''When? . . .''

''Early this month,'' Coke put in. ''They say the great man was at sea six weeks and scarcely escaped capture! He landed at Fréjus with a bare half dozen of an escort, and was greeted like a king. Fox was thinking of sending him a message of congratulation.''

There was silence. Ross held his tongue. Presently he said: ''Certainly, since Hoche died, Buonaparte stands alone. The French armies no doubt will look on him as their saviour.''

''Which it's doubtful if he can be,'' said Crutchley, who, like Ross, supported Pitt and the war effort. ''While he's been bottled up in Egypt, all his conquests in Europe have been lost. Now we have a firm foothold in Holland it will be no time before Russia joins us there. Nearly all the French possessions overseas are in our hands: Ceylon, all of southern India, the Cape of Good Hope, Minorca, Trinidad. The best that their 'saviour' can do is rally the defeated armies and sue for peace.''

''There's been a great bungling of our efforts in the Helder,'' said Coke, with some satisfaction. ''More determination would have given us the whole of Holland by now.''

''If Abercrombie had not been forced to use his raw militia last week — ''

''Gentlemen,'' Caroline said. ''Mr. St. John is right. The supper table is for light talk, however weighty the platters we put on it. This *soirée* you have been to: was it an interesting evening?''

III

They stayed late, drinking and laughing and talking. It had been a long day in the open air and Demelza's eyes were pricking with sleep long before they finally said good night and took two hackney chairs home. Ross had been slow to leave, and she could not know that it was a part of his design that she should be tired and sleep late in the morning.

When she lay in bed at last she talked for a moment or two about the Strawberry

Hill garden and all the fascinating things there were in it. No one in Cornwall, it seemed to her, had begun to lay out a garden like this. There was a small formal garden at Tregothnan, and splendid landscaping had been done at places like Tehidy and Trelissick. But this was *small* landscaping, within the compass of a few acres; superbly arranged trees of all shapes, sizes, and colours; golden bushes, blue pyramids, grey towering sentinels, with all the profusion of flowering plants set between and showing them off. Where did you *get* such trees and shrubs: where did you *buy* them; did you have to order them from the Indies and Australia and America? Ross answered yes, and no, and I have little idea, and perhaps we can inquire. He should, he knew, have warned her again that not a quarter of the plants she coveted would stand the sandy soil and salt-laden winds of the north Cornish coast; but for the moment he had not the heart. He waited until she had fallen asleep, and then he quietly undressed and slid into bed beside her and lay for a long time, hands behind head, staring up at the ceiling.

He had arranged to be wakened at five; and he rose and by the light of a shaded candle washed and shaved and brushed and combed his hair. It was still pitch dark outside, and was likely still to be so at six. He supposed that by the time the preliminaries had been gone through dawn would be breaking. One presumably had to be able to *see* one's opponent.

He had never himself fought a duel before, but he had been second to a brother officer in New York when he had quarrelled with a lieutenant in another regiment, and they had fought it out in the fields behind the encampment. Both had been severely wounded. Even then, when he was himself only twenty-two and more romantically inclined, he had thought the whole procedure an exaggerated and outdated way of settling differences. In the camp of that time there was an average of one duel every week, and frequently good men killed; and he knew that although decrees had been issued by both the civilian and the military authorities, the frequency of such affrays had scarcely dropped since then.

Often the dispute was of the lightest, some joke misinterpreted. Dwight was wrong in supposing his disagreement with Adderley too trivial for such a resolution. Only last March when he was in London there had been a quarrel in Stephenson's Hotel in Bond Street. Viscount Falkland had been drinking there with some friends, among them a Mr. Powell, and Falkland had merely said: "What, drunk again, Pogey?" whereupon Powell had made a sharp reply and Falkland had hit him with a cane. In the resultant duel Falkland, a man of forty-one, had been shot dead. So it went on, and so it would go on. But he had not supposed that he himself would ever be involved in such an affray.

Long years ago he had made a will, and it was deposited with Mr. Pearce — and would now presumably have been passed on among all the other boxes of legal documents to whoever was taking over the remnants of Mr. Pearce's devastated practice — but that had been done before the children were born, when he had been about to be tried for his life in Bodmin.

He supposed he should have made some later attempt to set his affairs in order. He knew one or two Cornishmen who made a fresh will whenever they set out for London.

Well, it was too late now. In less than an hour the matter would be decided. At five forty-five he heard the clop of hooves. Most of the lamps in the narrow sloping street had gone out for lack of fish oil, but the few left showed that Dwight, for all his angry protests, was not late for his appointment.

Ross glanced at the sleeping figure of his wife. Her face was half hidden and he decided not to make any attempt to touch her, for she was quick to wake. He put on his cloak and hat, tiptoed to the door, which creaked maddeningly, and then, guttering candle in hand, went down the stairs. At the outer door he blew out the candle, put it on a ledge, and stepped into the street.

The air was cold, and a light drizzle was falling. Ross mounted the other horse that Dwight had brought, and stared at his friend.

"Did you have any difficulty? . . ."

Dwight said: "Only the difficulty of believing that so rational a man as yourself, and my best and oldest friend, should indulge in such madness and pursue it to the bitter end."

Ross said: "Unless the sky lightens soon there will be more danger to the birds in the trees. Or do we hold a torch in our left hand?"

Dwight said: "Even by the absurd standards of today, this meeting is ridiculously irregular. As challenger Adderley must give you choice of weapons. Yet before you even consult me you accept all his terms."

"Because they suit me. I have never used a sword except in practice with the regiment seventeen years ago. At least with a pistol I have a very good idea what happens when the trigger is pulled."

"*Did* you take some practise yesterday morning?"

"Yes, with a sergeant at the Savoy. His chief advice, however, seemed to be 'Watch how you load the pistol, sir: too much gunpowder destroys the equilibrium, too much velocity affects the precision of the ball. If anything, sir, it is better to undercharge.' Since you will be in command of the pistols and not I, I can only pass on this gem of wisdom for your attention."

They turned and began to move up the hill. They rode along the Strand and up Cockspur Street and the Hay Market to Piccadilly, thence to Hyde Park Corner. There were a few shadowy figures still skulking about, seeking whom or what they might pick up or rob. As their horses turned up Tyburn Lane the watch was ringing his bell and calling: "Past six o'clock and all's well." It was his last call before he went home. In the Park although there was no wind the leaves were falling regularly like some too conventional stage set. The rain had just stopped. In the dim light there seemed no one about when they reached the ring, and, for the five minutes they sat there while their horses' nostrils steamed in the still morning, Dwight had time to hope that Adderley had thought better of his challenge. But presently there was the clop of a hoof and the snort of a restive horse, and two figures loomed up in the semi-dark.

"As God is my judge," said Monk, erect as a lancer. "I thought you'd run home to Cornwall."

"As God is my judge," said Ross, "I thought you were going to plead benefit of clergy."

It was not a good beginning on which to base a move of reconciliation, but as they rode further into the trees Dwight drew Craven aside, and after they had dismounted there was a further conference. In the meantime Ross paced slowly across the clearing they had chosen, hands behind back, taking deep breaths of the fresh morning, listening to the occasional sleepy chirrup of a waking bird. Adderley stood quite still, like one of those thin pencil trees Demelza had so admired yesterday.

There was now a faint glimmer of light showing from over in the direction of the city. The air was fresh here, with none of the town smells to pollute it. The leaves squelched under Ross's feet. Dwight came across. His face looked thin.

"I've agreed with Craven that the light will be good enough in twenty minutes. We have that time still to come to some accommodation."

"I want no accommodation," said Ross.

"God curse it!" Dwight said, and it was rare for him to swear; "have *neither* of you any sense? The bloodletting will solve nothing!"

"Let us walk," Ross said. "The morning air is chill, and warm blood makes for a steady hand."

They began to walk through the trees, a hundred yards this way, a hundred back again.

Ross said: "Let us not dramatise the situation, Dwight; but if by chance his aim is better than mine, you and Caroline, as our close friends, will bear a responsibility for the future of those in Nampara."

"Of course."

"There is nothing writ. It will all have to be understood."

"It is understood."

Time passed slowly. Ross remembered

a story he had heard somewhere of two men who had challenged each other to a duel, and they happened to be dining together at one of their houses in a great company of society. Having dined and spent the evening and supped, they left at one, and each rode to the rendezvous in his own coach and sat there in the dark, till six, when they got out and shot each other to death.

Trees at last were assuming definition; and in the distance the shape of buildings could be seen. Fortunately with the end of the rain had come a break in the clouds, so that as sunrise neared the day broke suddenly.

Dwight said: "Come, it is time."

CHAPTER VI

They came together and while the pistols were examined and loaded Dwight made one more effort.

"Captain Adderley, I think it is acknowledged even by you that at the time of this disagreement in the House Captain Poldark apologised for his brief loss of temper. That is the act of a gentleman and it would equally be the act of a gentleman if you were now to accept it. Why do you not both shake hands and go home to a hearty breakfast? No one knows of this encounter except yourselves. At your request it has been kept secret. Therefore there is no honour to be maintained in the face of other people. There is nothing to lose and everything to gain by looking on this as a superficial quarrel not worthy of bloodshed."

Adderley's macabre face looked as if it had spent all its time in the dark. "If Captain Poldark will apologise again now, and undertake to send me a written apology couched in suitable terms, I might consider it. Though I should think ill of him if I did so."

Dwight looked at Ross.

Ross said: "My only regret was that I apologised in the first place."

Dwight made a gesture of despair, and Craven said: "Come, gentlemen, we are wasting time. It should all be over before sunup."

"One thing," Adderley said. "I take it that your second has given to mine the letter of challenge that I wrote you."

"Yes. You asked for it."

"And mine has given to yours your reply. So there is no evidence as to the occurrence of this duel, except for the presence of these two men, who are sworn to secrecy. The noise of the pistols may attract attention even at this early hour, so if I should kill you or wound you I shall waste no time in inquiring into your injuries but shall mount and ride away as quick as I can. If by mischance you should injure me instead you have my full permission to do the same. And the injured party has been set upon by a highwayman."

"Agreed," Ross said.

"I would hate," Adderley said, "to languish in gaol for shedding *your* blood, my dear."

So they stood back to back. They were both tall men, and much of a height, but Ross the bigger-boned. Pistols in hand; one in each hand, loaded and primed. Too much gunpowder destroys the equilibrium, sir. If anything, sir, it is better to undercharge. Too much velocity affects the precision of the shell. Was this fear one felt? Not quite. A keyed-up will for violence, to destroy something that was half in the other man, half in oneself. To fire. To fire. Imagination stopped. So did apprehension. Flesh and its frailty was not as important as will and its integrity. One put all one's future on the table for the throw of a die. Heart pounding but hands calm, eyes clear, senses over-acute, smell of wood smoke, sound of a distant bell.

"Fourteen paces," said Craven. "I will count. *Now.* One, two, three."

The paces were slow as his count was slow.

". . . Thirteen, fourteen. Attend. Present. Fire!"

They both fired simultaneously and it seemed both missed. The light was still not too good. Ross had heard the ball go past.

"That will do!" Dwight said, moving forward.

Adderley dropped the empty pistol and changed hands, raised the other. As he saw this Ross did the same. Just as he fired the pistol was knocked out of his hand and he felt a searing pain in his forearm. To his surprise the force of the ball had swung him round. He half doubled, clutching his arm, and then through the smoke saw Adderley on the ground.

Blood was oozing through his fingers in great thick gushes. Dwight was beside him, was trying to tear the rest of the torn sleeve away.

"Adderley," Ross said. "You'd best

go and see — "

"In a moment. You must get that — "

"Dr. Enys!" Craven was plucking at his coat. "Captain Adderley is serious wounded."

"Go on," said Ross, as Dwight hesitated.

Dwight said: "Get something round your upper arm quick as you can — else you'll bleed to death."

Ross sat down on a stone and tried to tear a piece of his shirt; it wouldn't give; eventually a piece of lace came away, and though it was thin it was strong. He wound this below his biceps with his left hand and then, unable to tie it, just twisted and twisted till it grew very tight. Then he could only hold it there. His forearm was a mess. Could not see if the ball had smashed the bone, but he had lost the use of his fingers. The trees were moving in an odd way, and it was all he could do not to keel over onto the damp, sere leaves.

The three men were over there in a group — could not be more than thirty paces away — clearly. Had he hit with his first or his second shot? And if so, how good (or bad) had been his aim? He gritted his teeth, got up. Arm was still bleeding but it was not *gushing* out. More blood than he'd ever lost from his two wounds in America. He began to walk.

Just like pacing out for the duel, only twice as far. Long way. Twenty-eight paces. Adderley was stirring. That was good thing. Not dead. Not dead. As he came up John Craven suddenly left the group, went running off through the trees towards the gate of the park.

Dwight had his bag and had cut away Adderley's coat and shirt and waistcoat, was holding a pad of gauze. It seemed to be at the base of the stomach, or the top of the right leg. Ross swayed up to them.

Adderley's eyes fluttered. "Damned pistols," he muttered. "Not . . . accurate. Damn near missed you altogether . . . my dear."

Ross said: "Where's Craven gone?"

"To get a chair," Dwight said.

"Didn't . . . ride . . ."

"He thought it quicker. There's usually

chairs by the toll gate. Look, sit down here. Then if you can hold this pad on Adderley's thigh with your left hand I can tie your arm."

"Hold the pad myself," Adderley said. "You get off, Poldark. While the going's good. That's — what we agreed."

"I'll stay till the chair comes," Ross said.

"Damn fool," said Adderley. "I knew it. Wish I'd *killed* you. No room for damned fools."

Ross squatted on the grass and held the pad over Monk's stomach, while Dwight tied up his arm. It was done with much speed and efficiency, and after a few minutes Dwight was able to slacken the tourniquet he had first put on.

"Can you ride home?" he asked.

"I — suspect so."

"Then go. Adderley's right. Craven might come back with a couple of the watch."

"Shoot him if he does," said Adderley.

"He might have no choice."

"I'll stay till the chair comes," Ross said obstinately.

Shafts of early sunlight were touching the tops of the trees. The faded leaves, still damp, were lit up with brass spears. Monk was only half conscious now. Ross looked at Dwight inquiringly. Dwight made a noncommittal gesture.

They waited.

Leaves continued to fall, making eccentric landings on the trio of silent men. Running feet, and Craven came into view followed by a hackney chair. Panting, the chairmen set the chair down, and with great difficulty Monk Adderley was lifted into it. He seemed at this stage to have fainted altogether.

Dwight said: "Mr. Craven, I'll go with this chair. Do you help Captain Poldark to mount and then bring the other horses."

Ross said: "I think I'll come with you."

"No," said Craven. "Fair's fair, and the conditions have been properly observed. So observe the rest. I advise you to go home and send for another physician."

While the chair moved off, Craven somehow pushed Ross up onto his horse, and with his bad arm held in a temporary sling, Ross gathered the reins and turned his horse quietly round to begin what was going to be an interminable journey to George Street.

II

By nine Dwight was round. He found Ross in bed but unattended, since he had refused to see any other physician. Demelza was doing what she could for him. She was looking more sick than Dwight had ever seen her since she had had the morbid sore throat.

"Well," said Ross. "What of Adderley?" and gritted his teeth while Dwight cut away the bandage.

"I've extracted the ball, which had lodged almost in the groin. Lead is sterile and I have taken what precautions I can."

There was silence while he examined the wound.

"Well?"

"It could be worse. The ball has split a splinter off the radius. I'll have to take that piece of bone out. The ulna is sound."

"Damned if I know whether I hit him with the first or the second shot."

"The second. The blow on your arm deflected your arm fractionally down. Demelza, have you a bowl?"

"Here."

"A bigger one. And brandy. This will be more painful than it should be, Ross, because if it had been done at once the shocked arm would still have been partly insensitive."

"I don't want brandy," Ross said. "Just do what you have to do."

So Dwight did what he had to do, and there was a lot of blood, and a moment when he had to saw the edge of the splintered bone. And sweat ran down Ross's face and he gripped the bed with his good hand until the rail bent, and there were sweat and tears on Demelza's face, and then presently the bandages were going back, and Demelza, anxious to keep everything as secret as possible, was carrying the bloody bowls out herself, and Dwight was closing his bag. And then they all sat and did drink brandy. And there was a long silence between them. The few words that were dropped into the silence did not keep it at bay. They had all retreated into their own thoughts: wry, bitter, anxious, recollective. Outside, London was full awake, and the customary noises in the street were temporarily joined by the lowing of a cow. Upstairs two maids were busy: you could hear their footsteps on the floor.

At length Dwight tried to break the sour spell.

"Have you ever heard of a man called Davy?"

Ross looked up. "Who?"

"Davy. Humphrey Davy, I think he's called."

"No," He made an effort. "Who is he?"

"A Cornish youth working in some laboratory in Bristol. He claims to have discovered — or invented — some new gas called nitrous oxide which he says induces insensibility when the fumes are breathed. The man is not yet twenty-one, but has already published his findings. He claims that, as the gas is capable of destroying pain, it may probably be used to advantage in surgical operations. I could have wished for some now."

"So could I have," said Ross.

Dwight got up.

"No doubt even if his claims be true it will be years before my profession puts it to the test. We are nothing if not conservative in our ideas."

There was a further oppressive silence.

"Is the pain easier?" Demelza asked.

"A little," said Ross. "Do you know, I have been considering. However much Adderley may have wished to keep this secret, it seems very likely to come out, now we are both in this condition."

Demelza looked at Ross, his drawn face, the blood already seeping through the new bandage. And she thought: I shall never forgive him for this.

III

And she thought it all the following days. To her it seemed like a blasphemy against life, to risk so much for so little. It showed a newer, darker side of Ross than even she had ever known. But also it showed a person bound by a foolish tradition of his class that he of all people should have been clear-sighted enough to disavow.

He was so introspective, and anyway so ill for a few days, that she could not bring herself to say anything to him, and the only person she could unburden herself to was Caroline.

Caroline said: "I was surprised myself — and yet, looking at it now, I am not surprised. It was always — on the cards."

"I don't know what you mean."

Caroline steered away from explaining. "Monk Adderley's a fighter. He will be all his days. It was just misfortune that he chose Ross."

Demelza's dark eyebrows wrinkled and contracted painfully. "That is not what you meant at all, Caroline. And it is not what I mean. They speak of honour. Honour having to be satisfied. What is honour?"

"A code of conduct. A long tradition. Ross would have lost respect if he had not fought."

"Respect? Whose respect? Not mine. And what else might he not have lost which is a small matter more important? His life? His health? We don't know even yet if those are safe. His wife, his children, his home, his career? What are those compared to respect?"

"Men are like that."

"I don't want men who are like that! Four years ago, Caroline, Ross risked all this before — to recover Dwight from Quimper prison in France. *That* is what I call honour. This I call dishonour!"

Caroline looked at her friend. "Go kindly with him, Demelza. You know him better than I; but if I read him right he will not escape his own self-criticism over this affair."

"So he should not! . . . But, Caroline, I feel so much of it is my fault."

"Your fault!"

"Well, my responsibility, like. It was over me. The quarrel was *really* over me. You know that, don't you."

"I know it was *partly* over you. But I do not believe it would have got so far on that alone. Ross and Monk detested each other from the moment they laid eyes on each other, and that is something in the blood, not a matter of behaviour."

Demelza got up. "*Was* my behaviour at fault?"

"None that I saw."

"You see, I was — happy. Ross and I were happier together than we had been since — since before Hugh; and I was excited, *enjoying* myself in a new society. Perhaps I was freer with Monk Adderley than I ought to have been. Maybe I'm too *free* for London society. Maybe men — anywhere — take too much encouragement from my manner, even in Cornwall. But it's the way I was *born*. Of course in all these years I've learned a lot, but maybe I haven't learned enough. Ross should never have brought me!"

"My dear, you can't make a general principle out of a single mishap. You could have come to London twenty times without this happening! Take heart that it's no worse. One or both of them might have been dead."

Demelza said: "That's what I think every minute of the day."

And then Monk Adderley died.

IV

Ross's fever was abating by the third day, and he was just making plans to get up, much against Demelza's wishes, to call on his adversary when John Craven arrived with the news.

Ross stared at him in grey silence, lying back on the pillows from which he had just part risen. Demelza, by the window, bit the back of her hand.

Craven said: "His own doctor was with him two hours before, and Dr. Enys visited him last eve, but there was nothing to be done. There appeared, Dr. Enys said, to have been some blockage in a blood vessel."

"When? . . . ."

"This forenoon." John Craven brushed a hand across the arm of his tidy jacket, glanced at Demelza and then away. "I came to tell you because that was what he wished. And to warn you."

"Yes. I see that."

"He has given it out that he was

practising with his pistols in the Park, when one of them was accidentally discharged into his stomach. This I will confirm."

"Thank you, Mr. Craven."

"Don't thank me, Captain Poldark. It comes distasteful in me to condone a lie and indeed to call in question my own honour in so doing."

"Then do not do it."

"Dr. Enys and myself were both sworn to this before the duel began. As it turned out, it may be necessary to go further than we had ever expected; but that is not your fault but the fault of the undertaking."

"Then I'll release you from it."

"Ross — "

Mr. Craven looked again at Demelza. "Have no fear, ma'am. I don't think he can release us from it, even if he so chooses. The man who could do that is dead."

No one spoke.

Craven said: "Captain Adderley also told me to tell you — and here I simply pass on his message, sir — that you were a damned fool to stay in the Park until the chairmen came; so there could be two witnesses that another man, also wounded, was in the vicinity. You are obviously, sir, in no position yet to hide your own wound. However, Captain Adderley instructed me to pay each of the chairmen five guineas to stop his mouth, and I think this will be sufficient.''

Ross swallowed and licked his lips. ''I was this moment about to come and see him. I wished to go yesterday but Dr. Enys said I must not move for another day. Now . . .''

Craven coughed. ''Captain Adderley said I must point out to you that you now owed him ten guineas.''

Ross stared. ''Well, of course; do you wish me to — ''

''He said it was not to go into his estate but requested that it be paid to Mr. George Warleggan in settlement of a wager.''

Demelza turned sharply from the window, but decided to say nothing.

Ross said: ''A wager in which I was involved?''

''Not necessarily, sir. I have no idea what the subject of the wager was.''

Two women were screaming at each other in the street outside, and further down hand bells were being rung by a variety of hawkers.

Ross said: "I take it Captain Adderley had no dependants, Mr. Craven?"

"None. He left a one-line will in which he said he left everything he owned to Miss Andromeda Page."

Ross grimaced as he moved his bad arm.

"I'm much indebted to you, Mr. Craven. Can we offer you a brandy? There's little else."

"Thank you, no. I must be on my way. I have to tell Dr. Enys. There will be an inquest tomorrow."

"Of course I will be present."

"Of course you must not. That would defeat the whole object of the conditions for the duel laid down by Captain Adderley from the beginning. As I have said, I do not fancy any part in this affair — certainly not my own."

"The fact that I did not see him before he died, to make this matter up, is something I shall regret for the rest of my life."

Craven shrugged. "Well, Captain Poldark, it was a fair fight, fairly conducted. I can vouch for that. You have nothing to reproach yourself with. Monk Adderley was a strange man, given to excess. I have to tell you that though he bore you not the slightest ill-will for the mortal wound you inflicted on him, one of his last remarks to me was 'I wish I'd killed that man.' "

V

The coroner's inquest was held in the upper room of the Star Garter Inn, Pall Mall. Demelza had wanted to go and listen but Dwight said no. The less sign of any connection with Captain Adderley, the better it would be. So she stayed with Ross at home and waited to be told what happened.

It took about an hour. The first witness was a Mrs. Osmonde, Adderley's landlady, who testified to his arrival home at seven-thirty one morning with a severe wound in the groin. He was brought in by two chairmen and was accompanied by

Mr. Craven and Dr. Enys. Captain Adderley then retired to his bed, she said, having told her that he had shot himself accidentally while practising with his pistol in Hyde Park. He had also made a sworn statement to this effect and she had been one of the witnesses to his signature. Mr. Craven was then called to the witness box and said that he had been out riding in the early morning and had heard a shot. He had ridden in the direction of the sound and found his friend Captain Adderley lying on the ground bleeding from a body wound. He had at once gone for two chairman, and on the way had met Dr. Enys, who had come back with him to the injured man, and had given him temporary treatment until they could get him home. He confirmed Mrs. Osmonde's further testimony, and had been the other witness to Adderley's statement. Answering the coroner, he agreed that Captain Adderley was a noted duellist but denied that he knew of any assignation that morning. Further questioned, he stated that there was no one else but Adderley on the scene when he arrived.

Dr. Enys was then called, and testified that he had been brought into Hyde Park by Mr. Craven and had attended on the wounded man on the spot, and later at his lodgings until the time of his death. "Was there no one else about when you arrived to attend to the wounded man?" the coroner asked. Dr. Enys hesitated fractionally, licked his lips, and then said: "No, sir." Dr. Corcoran followed him into the box and confirmed Dr. Enys's report that Captain Adderley had died from the effects of a pistol ball which had wounded him in the groin and later caused a seizure of the blood vessels and cardiac failure. "Could this wound have been self-inflicted?" the coroner asked, a question he had failed to put to Dwight. Dr. Corcoran said he considered it unlikely but not impossible. Dr. Enys was then recalled and asked the same question. Dr. Enys said he thought it was possible.

The coroner then asked if the two chairmen had been traced; but they had not; indeed, it seemed that they had vanished, and none knew their names. The jury retired and were out ten minutes.

They brought in a verdict of "Death by Misadventure."

Yet almost by the time the inquest was taking place it had become common knowledge in parliamentary and social circles as to what had happened. No one knew how it had leaked out. There was of course the brief fracas in the House. Perhaps Adderley had said something to Andromeda Page. It then just remained a moot point as to whether the authorities would decide to move against the survivor — whether if they did there was any sort of proof more substantial than "common" knowledge. Ross was determined to go to Adderley's funeral, and it took Dwight's brute force to prevent him. To go to the funeral might invite an insult or an outburst from one of Monk's friends; it would in any event certainly invite comment.

Fortunately, from this point of view, he was still very unwell, and only sat up in his chamber for an hour or two each day. His wounds in America, while in a way more serious, had scarcely incommoded him more. Dwight watched the arm with anxiety. It was refusing to heal.

Demelza forced herself to catechise Ross on what his attitude would be if a constable or some other representative of the law called on them. At first he had said that he could only answer the questions. When she had asked him if he would answer truthfully or untruthfully he had replied that it depended on what he was asked. This did not satisfy her, and she put question after question to him to see what he would say. It wasn't very satisfactory until she asked him what was the point of two honourable men perjuring themselves on his behalf if at the end of it he was going to despise their help?

So one day slowly followed another, and they both sat indoors waiting for the official knock.

CHAPTER VII

In his own twisted way Adderley had played the game with his opponent until the very end, so that George Warleggan did not even hear of his wound until the Thursday. He went round to Adderley's lodgings on the Friday morning, to find the curtains already drawn and a landlady going on with her work while she waited for the boy to come back with Dr. Corcoran to pronounce life extinct. Even then it took time to elicit the facts. He went along to the inquest, still not sure of them, but suspecting what might have happened. Whispered gossip confirmed his suspicions during the next few days, and he was furious to feel that Adderley's adversary might escape the law.

On the Monday following he called on Mr. Henry Bull, K.C., at his office in

Westminster. Nine years ago Mr. Bull had been concerned as leader for the Crown in a case in Cornwall where a man had been on trial for his life on a charge of riot, inciting others to riot and to wreck, and for assault on a customs officer. At that time George had got to know Mr. Bull, and since then had kept in touch with him as he watched his rise to a position of influence. He was now King's Advocate, which meant he was the principal law officer of the Crown in the admiralty and ecclesiastical courts.

He seemed to George the most suitable person to approach — the most suitable whom he knew, that was — and Mr. Bull, aware of Mr. Warleggan's growing power and influence, was careful to welcome him with a due display of courtesy and attention. With courtesy and attention he heard Mr. Warleggan state his complaint.

"Well, yes," he said. "Of course I remember Poldark well. Stiff-necked fellow. He should have hanged then if justice had been done, but your Cornish juries are too sentimental to their own. But this case, sir, this case — even if everything that's whispered be true, where's your evidence? Eh? Eh? The inquest's been held, the verdict's Death by Misadventure. To overset that we should need some fresh evidence to corroborate all this talk."

"Poldark has been wounded and is confined to his apartment. That is common knowledge."

"Yes. True enough. But it's only an inference that there is a connection. People may be jumping to conclusions."

"At least he should be interrogated."

"He could be. But I'm not certain on what grounds, eh? No one 'ias actually *accused* him of anything. Adderley's dead. No one saw Poldark in Hyde Park that morning. Or if they did they've lied to save his skin. Looks to me there must have been some sort of pact. All very irregular, but y'know Adderley's been in more trouble than Poldark — at least so far as duelling is concerned — I would suppose they agreed to fight it out between themselves without seconds, nobody there at all, devil take the one who fell. Most irregular, I must say: not the way gentlemen should behave. But they're two army men; infantry at that; both mad as Ajax; what can you expect?"

"To me," said George, "it is outrageous to suppose that his great friend Craven should 'just have been passing' at the time of the shot. Also that Dr. Enys should be out in that area so early in the morning. No attempt — virtually no attempt — has been made to trace the chairmen who bore Adderley home. Nor any attempt to find any other witnesses to the scene. The whole thing stinks of contrivance, sir!"

"May be. May be." Mr. Bull pursed his thick lips and stared at the papers in front of him. "Well, Mr. Warleggan, happy as I should be to help — though it's not really my territory — there's little *official* action I can suggest at this stage. If unofficial inquiries should uncover some promising information I shall be glad to hear it and to forward it to the correct quarters."

With that George had to be content for the time being, but on his regular attendances at White's, where he had been careful to go three times a week since his election, he had noticed that Sir John

Mitford, the Attorney General, was a member. George knew him by sight but no more; but he had already spotted a member who knew everyone and who was short of money and keen to befriend those who had much of it, so one evening he laid in wait, and after seeing Sir John go into the smoking room after dinner, he called on his new friend to contrive an introduction.

Presently it was done. Mitford accepted the introduction with a good grace, and after a few moments of casual talk the third man faded out.

So George was able to run the conversation tactfully in the direction he wanted, and remarked how much the club must be feeling the loss of one of its most popular members. Who was that? asked Mitford; ah, yes, and his eyebrows came together, ah, yes, young Adderley, something of a pity, though the fellow could never play a fair hand of whist without turning it into an outrageous gamble. George said he particularly regretted the loss because Monk Adderley in fact had been his proposer in the club, and was an old and valued friend. After a few more such remarks the word "murder" got itself inserted into the conversation. Murder? said Sir John, who says so? The verdict was Misadventure. George smiled and said, oh, yes, sir, but nobody believes that.

"Ah," said Mitford, "you mean this story of a duel? It's current, I know. What is the name of the fellow whose name is linked with all this? Pol-something. Don't know that I've ever met him or know anything about him."

George gave a brief, loaded summary of Ross's career, with some detail of the charges brought against him in Bodmin and the general agreement that he was guilty of the indictment but had been freed by a prejudiced jury.

"Ah," said Mitford. "He sounds a bit of a rake-helly. But then so was Adderley. Little to choose between 'em, I should say. Pity they didn't kill each other."

"Well, Sir John, but they did *not,*" said George. "If I may venture to say so, should Poldark now go free, without even being *charged,* it would be a grave miscarriage of justice."

Mitford looked at the other man from under his eyebrows. "My dear Mr. Warlesson, I am not, as you will appreciate, able to keep an eye on all the day-to-day mishaps that occur in this metropolis. Nor is anyone else. The city is gravely underpoliced, as you must know. In the whole district of Kensington, for instance, there are only three constables and three head boroughs to police an area of fifteen square miles. What can you expect from that?" Sir John cleared his throat noisily. "But then, looking at it all the way round, who is to say Adderley did not take his own life deliberate? We know how hard drove he was for money. There's some in this club will never see the colour of their gold again. But even if it was as you say . . ."

"Yes? . . ."

"Adderley was not shot in the back, was he? No one's saying this fellow Pol-something didn't shoot him in fair fight?"

"Duelling is illegal in the eye of the law, Sir John. All the great authorities —

Coke, Bacon, and the rest — have stated that it differs nothing from ordinary murder. And this is worse, being a secretive assignation."

Sir John got up. "I have a business appointment, so I trust you'll excuse me, sir. As to the law of the land, it so happens that I am acquainted with it. If a man is killed in a duel, his opponent shall be indicted for murder. The law of the land, however, I would remind you, demands evidence as to fact. Gossip and suspicion are noticeably unreliable witnesses when they go into the box. When you have something more concrete to go on than the tittle-tattle of the drawing rooms, pray let me know."

On the way out to the gaming rooms Sir John looked at the list of new members posted in the fall in the hall to ascertain that Mr. Warlesson was on it.

So George paid two men to make further inquiries, and Ross continued to nurse his wound while Demelza waited.

II

They had a fair number of visitors. The fiction that he had shot himself while priming his pistol was elaborately maintained and talk was of the failure, after all the high hopes, of the campaign in Holland, of the bitterness and suspicion between the Russians and the English as an outcome, of the fact that Russians who had landed at Yarmouth were drinking the oil out of the street lamps, of the acclaim with which General Buonaparte was being greeted in France, of the hopes of peace and of the weariness of the eight-year war. Or they talked of the latest play, the latest scandal, or the latest rumours as to the King's health. Nothing more personal at all.

And through it all, in the back of Demelza's mind, jingling now with a peculiar malevolence, ran the ditty whose tune she could not forget:

Shepherd, I have lost my
    waist,
Have you seen my body?

Sacrificed to modern taste,
I'm quite a Hoddy-Doddy . . .

There was one surprise visitor. When Mrs. Parkins gave in his name Demelza went to the door to make sure she had heard aright. It was Geoffrey Charles Poldark.

"Well, well, Aunt Demelza — looking so anxious! Do you suppose I am a ghost? May I be permitted to see my respected uncle?"

Pale and thin, he came in. Ross was sitting in a chair in a morning gown, his arm still throbbing, but feeling better in health. He smiled at the young man, and offered his left hand, but Geoffrey Charles bent and kissed him on the cheek. Then he kissed Demelza. He was dressed in a blue and brown striped silk cloth coat and breeches with a white silk waistcoat.

"Blister my tripes!" he said. "Uncle Ross, what is this I hear, that you have been shooting off your own hand? As God's my life I should never have guessed you could be anything so careless! And how is it? Part mended, I hope? Near as

730

good as new? Are you going to try your foot next, because I should advise against it. Feet are more painful.''

Ross said: "I'd warn you it is hazardous to jest with an invalid. My temper is very short. But what are you doing here — playing truant from your studies to become a fop?''

"What am I doing here? There's gratitude for you! I'm visiting a sick relative, that is what. Excuse enough to absent myself from any studies, ain't it?''

"We'll pass it this time," said Ross. "Demelza, could you pull the bell. The boy will be hungry.''

"I find it very diverting," Geoffrey Charles said, "at my age, that everyone assumes, as it were takes for granted, that I am always hungry.''

"And aren't you?''

"Yes.''

They all laughed.

"Serious, though," said Ross, when tea and crumpets and buttered scones had been ordered.

"Serious, now that Ma-ma and Uncle George are living in King Street, it is really

731

no distance for me to come down, so I often take an afternoon off and spend it with them — or at least with Ma-ma and Valentine, Uncle George being frequently out and about his businesses. So I thought, learning of your mishap, I would take the opportunity of calling upon you instead."

They chatted for a while, agreeably, a sudden lightness in the air for the first time since the duel.

Ross said: "I had intended bringing your aunt to see you, or inviting you, as now, to come and see us; but you'll appreciate that as your uncle George and I . . . well, I hesitate to make any move that might upset — your mother."

"Ah," said Geoffrey Charles. *"Dicenda tacenda locutus.* Do you know, Aunt Demelza, one spends hours learning stupid languages solely to enable one to appear superior to those who have never been able to afford time. I would much rather be with Drake learning to make a wheel."

Demelza gave him one of her brilliant smiles.

"They do not know you are here,

then?'' Ross said.

"No. Nor shall they. Though in a short time I shall not give a tinker's curse what Uncle George thinks. In less than two years I shall be at Magdalen Collge, and then I shall feel pretty much my own master."

Ross moved his arm to ease the throbbing. "Geoffrey, you cannot come in for Trenwith for at least another three years. Then there is only property, no money. Without your uncle George to finance you the place would go to ruin — as it was going before your mother married him. So on all counts I'd advise you to exercise some discretion — not merely for your mother's sake but for your own. If when you are older — say in four or five years — you find it necessary for your own good health to break with Mr. Warleggan and to claim your inheritance absolutely, I shall have — by then I shall hope to have — enough money from the mine, and from other sources, to see you come into your inheritance not entirely penniless. But that is in the future. At present . . .''

Geoffrey Charles leaned back in his

chair and frowned. "Thank you, Uncle. That's very handsomely said. I hope I shall not need your help. Though God knows, my tastes already outrun my allowance. What a degrading subject money is! And how disagreeable that Stepfather George has so much of it! Can we not change the subject to something more savoury? Would you care, indeed — if it's not too delicate a subject — to tell me a little more of how you came to be shot in the hand?"

There was a pause. "No," said Ross.

"Ah. So that is not more savoury neither. . . . Aunt, you look nice enough to eat. On the whole London girls are prettier than Cornish girls. But just once in a while, you see one in our county that really takes the biscuit."

"Talking of biscuits," said Demelza, smiling at him again, "I think this is tea."

III

He left about seven, scorning Demelza's concern about his being safe in the streets of London. He had been given permission to spend the night at Grosvenor Gate, so there was no hurry. He walked up the street as far as the Strand, pushing his way through a group of prostitutes who plucked at his clothes and his body as he went past, and soon found a hackney chair.

When he reached home he found a pleasant family scene. George was home, and turning over a book — it looked like an accounts book — in front of a bright fire. Elizabeth was sitting on the other side looking as beautiful as ever, though Geoffrey Charles thought she was putting on weight. They had not told him yet. In a corner of the room Valentine Warleggan, not quite six years old, dark-haired, sallow-complexioned but good-looking in a thin angular way, was playing with his rocking horse. Elizabeth asked him how he had enjoyed the Zoo, and surely he had stayed too late? He replied that reptiles only wakened when night fell, and he had spent the last hour in the snake house. Lies came easily to him, he found, since he went to Harrow.

George welcomed him with amiability. To give George his due, he had always tried to treat his stepson with consideration. It was his stepson who refused to unbend. It was his stepson who refused to let bygones be bygones. Their relationship now was as good as it had ever been: a sort of polite toleration existed between them, which was about as much as Elizabeth dared to hope for.

In spite of the half-meant, half-malicious wager with Monk Adderley which had gone so badly awry, George was in a fair mood tonight. True, the men he had set to make inquiries had turned up yesterday with two chairmen who claimed to have been the men who bore the wounded Adderley to his lodgings; but a little close questioning of them soon proved they were lying and had only come forward to gain the reward George was offering: any lawyer in a court would have split them open in five minutes. So they had been sent about their business, and George's men too, with instructions to be more careful as to the quality of the fish they netted.

George was philosophical about it. With the death of Monk he had lost one of his most valuable social assets; but Monk while he was alive had been a heavy financial liability. He had had no care for money at all, and, since he became intimate with George, had tended to look on George as an inexhaustible supplier. One loan had followed another. Sometimes he had repaid a little, and then had borrowed all over again. So, though it was sad to lose him, it was not all loss. George fancied he could get along quite well enough on his own.

And even if the guilt for the killing were never laid firmly on Ross Poldark's shoulders, the result was still a fair one. Ross was at present laid up with a wound that they said would likely result in the loss of an arm; and in any event such an affray could do his career considerable disservice. The Boscawens, if George judged them right, were law-abiding above everything else, and they certainly would not want to be represented in Parliament by a firebrand who killed another member clandestinely, in a common duel, fought without even the proper formalities. As for the newly founded bank; news of the affray would travel swiftly to Cornwall; bankers too lived close within the law; it would likely damage him there also.

George's own affairs in other ways were prospering. Mr. Tankard, his personal lawyer and factor, had arrived in London yesterday with numerous documents and legal information. Now that he virtually owned the borough of St. Michael, George sought ways to render its possession less expensive.

There were in the borough about forty householders with sufficient of a dwelling to pay the poor rate. The fact that some of these dwellings were in such a bad state that they were almost falling down over their occupiers' heads did not prevent the householders from thus possessing a vote and capitalising on it. Such men would vote for whomever they were told, provided they received enough favours from the landlord. George was now the landlord. And he had found that the voters, though servile to a degree, were not easily satisfied with their requests. Getting oneself elected was of course the most expensive procedure, but it was by no means the only time at which they expected to benefit.

The scheme was simply to pull down some of the oldest and most derelict of the houses. It would take time, and perhaps a degree of firmness, but it could be done. For instance, the loss of ten houses would reduce his future costs by a quarter. Of course the inhabitants would vehemently object, but he had already bought a row of derelict cottages near a dead mine about two miles away and was having them repaired. No one could accuse him of inhumanity. The creatures he was moving were so indigent, and the houses he was moving them from were so poor, that he could even claim to be improving their lot. The only difference was that they would no longer be ratepayers in the parliamentary borough of St. Michael, and therefore their main livelihood would be gone. They might, George thought, even have to *work*.

He was at present examining the book

that Tankard had given him, which gave in detail the nature of the properties to be pulled down, the occupiers, their ages, and the dates by which each one, with his family or dependants, might be expected to get out.

Elizabeth said: "Valentine, it is time for your supper. I think Mrs. Wantage has forgotten you."

"Yes, Ma-ma. In two or three minutes, Ma-ma." Valentine was riding his rocking horse, whip in hand, a dark lock of hair hanging over his face. He was clearly engaged on some dangerous mission that must not be interrupted.

Geoffrey Charles was amused at him. "Ecod, I think Valentine's going to fight a duel."

"Thomas Trevethan, shoemaker," George read to himself. "Aged fifty-seven lives with widowed sister, Susan Hicks, fifty-nine." Already Trevethan had had a note sent to George asking for his patronage in the matter of boots and shoes. He would be well rid of. "Tom Oliver. Dairyman, aged forty, wife and four children." Dairyman for whom?

No doubt he kept one emaciated cow. "Arthur Pearson, maltster." What professions these parasites thought of!

Geoffrey Charles was laughing aloud. He laughed his high half-broken laugh, so that Elizabeth, smiling, lowered her needlepoint and George his book. Even Valentine lost his concentration and his horse began to rock less violently.

"What is it?" Elizabeth said. "What is it, Geoffrey Charles? What is amusing you so?"

"It's — it's Valentine!" Geoffrey Charles choked with amusement. "Just look at him! Ecod! Is he not the very spit and living image of Uncle Ross!"

CHAPTER VIII

On the ninth of November, Dwight gingerly unwrapped the bandages again, sniffing at them as they came away. They revealed an arm still inflamed, but only around the area of the wound. The swelling had gone down.

He said: "You're more lucky than you know, Ross."

"How so?"

"Three days ago I thought to amputate the arm above the elbow. There is a stage, as I'm sure you know, when the blood poisoning travels fast. Then it's a question of losing a limb to save a life."

"Don't tell Demelza."

"She already knows. I could not take the gamble without her permission."

Ross looked at his arm. "And now?"

Dwight was folding the bandage. "It

must have been dye from the sleeve that was carried in . . . Now? Oh, it should be good enough for most purposes in a month or so. Demelza will have to cut up your meat a while yet."

"I can scarce move my fingers."

"Don't try too hard. A little gentle exercise each morning. Ross, I'm returning to Cornwall next week. I only stayed this long because of you."

"Caroline is going with you?"

"No . . . There are some events she wishes to attend at the end of this month. She will return in early December."

"For longer this time, I hope."

Dwight put the bandage away and shut his bag. The morning light showed up his face as unexpectedly youthful under the greying hair.

"I think so. She says so."

Ross said: "At least, whatever value your visit has been to Caroline, it has very near saved my life."

"Your own body saved your life, Ross, because it was strong enough in the end to reject the infection."

"Stronger at least than my mind,

which could not resist the infection of Monk Adderley."

"It's over and done with, Ross; all that. You must think of the future, not of the past."

"I'm not so sure it's all over yet. An act like that carries its own consequences with it."

Dwight fumbled with the catch of his bag.

"Why do you not come home with me when I go?"

"No. Not yet. There are some things I must still do."

"You can't undo what's *been* done, Ross. It's a question of adjusting oneself to a new situation."

"Well, that we shall see . . ."

The following day fog was rising from the river as Ross waited upon his patron. He found Lord Falmouth at home and willing to receive him. They talked in a back parlour, since Mrs. Boscawen was entertaining ladies to tea in the drawing room.

Lord Falmouth had shaken Ross by the left hand and dryly suggested they should take a glass of canary. He was wearing a skullcap, a plum-coloured coat shiny at the elbows, and black silk knee breeches and stockings.

"I trust your . . . self-inflicted wound is healing."

"Thank you, my lord. It is. Though it has been long enough about it. Dr. Enys tells me that only time stands between me and my ability to sign my name again."

"That will be of use to you when you return to your banking friends."

"Always supposing they still wish to retain me."

Falmouth handed the glass to his guest. "You were fortunate to bring your own surgeon with you. It is a refinement even I have not felt able to afford."

Ross smiled. "He's returning at the beginning of next week. After which I shall have to fend for myself or call in some mere London man." He sipped the wine, and there was a pause. "A lot has happened since I dined with you last, Lord Falmouth."

"So I have observed."

It was difficult to read the Viscount's

expression. Never a man given to a show of feeling, he seemed now to be carefully avoiding it. His voice, apart from the little turn of sarcasm, was neutral, as if he waited for his visitor to declare his intent before committing himself to show his own.

"The story of what really happened is, I believe, well known by now," Ross said. "Yet it may be that the precise truth has not emerged in the telling; and I thought you should know it from me as soon as I was able to get out."

"If you're sure you wish to tell me."

"Why should I not be?"

"Because rumour is one thing, confession another. Some things are better left unsaid, Captain Poldark."

"I can assure you, my lord, that, except for this occasion, they will *remain* unsaid. But I represent Truro in your interest, and that interest, though I pay small heed to it sometimes, entitles you in this matter to know what was done."

"Very well." Falmouth went to the French windows, which looked out onto a conservatory, and shut them. "Say what you wish to say."

Ross told him the story of the duel. When it was done the other man refilled the glasses, frowning to see that none was spilled.

"So what do you want from me?"

"Possibly some advice."

"Of what sort?"

"I am known in Cornwall as a man of some temper. Now I am so known in London. The duel, of course, was fairly fought, but the mere fact that it was fought in a clandestine manner and that the law is not able to move against me — or *seems* not able to — gives it a shadier implication than if I were properly tried and served a sentence. You want someone to represent you in Westminster who is a parliamentarian, not a quarrelsome hothead. This stigma will linger in London for a while. I would have thought my proper course would be to resign my seat and for you to appoint someone more suitable in my place. After all, Truro is perfectly safe now and is entirely in your possession. There would be no need for an election. The matter could go through in a couple of months."

Lord Falmouth got up and pulled the bell. A manservant came.

"Bring me a bottle of the older canary."

"Yes, m'lord."

"And take this empty one."

"Yes, m'lord."

Silence prevailed until the new wine came.

"This is better," Falmouth said. "It has a smoky flavour on the tongue. Alas, there's little more of it. My mother got it last year."

"Yes," Ross said. "It has more body."

"As for you problem, Poldark, are you telling me you are tired of Westminster and wish to leave anyway?"

"That was not what I said. But I think it may be, in the year or so I have sat in Parliament, that you have tired of me."

His Lordship nodded his head. "That may be. We have not infrequently been at variance. But only in one or two matters — such as the Catholic Emancipation Bill — has there been a difference on an important issue. Where our differences *really* occur are not on issues but on principles."

"I'm not quite sure what you mean."

"Well, let us instance a single matter. You dislike what the French revolution has become and are prepared to fight it with all means in your power. But at heart I think you believe in the fundamentals of Liberty, Equality, and Fraternity yourself, though do not see it in those terms or say it in those words. Your humanity, your sentiment, respond to it and they are not sufficiently governed by your head, which would tell you that the achievement of those aims is impossible!"

Ross was silent for a while. "But if you take the emotion — the republicanism — the sense of violent revolution — out of them, do you not feel drawn to such ideals yourself?"

Falmouth smiled, tight-lipped. "Perhaps I have better trained myself, always to be governed by my head. Shall I say that I believe greatly in Fraternity, something in Liberty, and not at all in Equality."

"Which is precisely the opposite of what the French have now done," Ross said. "They have insisted so much on Equality that there is no room left for Liberty and little for Fraternity. But you haven't answered my question."

"Then I'll answer it now." His lordship paced about the room for a few moments, and took off his skullcap to scratch his head. "When I want you to resign I will tell you so. And when you wish to resign pray tell me. I like *some* character in a member, you know. But a stupid and unfortunately fatal affair of honour, much as it should be deplored, is not the grounds for such a decision. We all learn by our mistakes. I try to. I trust you will, Captain Poldark."

Ross put down his glass. "Thank you. That's what I wished to know."

"But go home," said Falmouth. "Go home at once. There's nothing important you can do here. And you know what the ancients said: 'When a man shall have been taken from sight he quickly goes also out of the mind.' This applies equally to the law. If they think of questioning you they may well do it if you are in George Street, but certainly will not travel three hundred miles to interview you on your estate in Cornwall.''

''I see that.''

''Then go tomorrow, or as soon as you can decently dispose of your affairs here.''

Ross thought for a long moment. ''My lord, I appreciate your thoughts for my welfare. It's considerate of you. . . . But I couldn't absent myself at this stage. I couldn't *skulk* away.''

Viscount Falmouth shrugged. ''There it is, Poldark. Once again we disagree. And once again on a matter of principle. You must be logical in life — not emotional.''

II

So it was time to go out and about again, into the public eye, in the Commons, into society. This in a way was the acid test. Adderley had few friends but many acquaintances. He was a ''figure'' who had been seen everywhere. Now he was seen nowhere. In his place, as it were, was the tall Cornishman with arm in sling, sometimes, when appropriate, accompanied by his pretty wife. Newcomers, strangers. Of course Mrs. Pelham had them under her wing, but . . . Adderley was missed. There were side glances, whisperings in the background, conversations that dried up when certain people approached.

To Ross's surprise, the Commons was easier. The members seemed to take it as a matter of course that an inveterate duellist would sooner or later come to his end by the means he himself employed. Their chief reaction was increased respect for the man who had killed him. Either Poldark was demmed good shot, as the member for Bridgnorth put it, or else he had been demmed lucky.

During all that very tense and disagreeable week the Hoddy-Doddy song kept repeating itself in Demelza's head, "Shepherd, I have lost my waist, Have you seen my body?" Unforgettable in spite of its complete, inane irrelevance to all her thoughts and fears.

Once they caught sight of George and Elizabeth at a *soirée,* and Ross bethought himself of Adderley's strange request.

It was something that had to be fulfilled, however difficult and embarrassing the action was going to be. Yet it must be inappropriate to hand George ten guineas in view of a roomful of people, and George might well think an insult intended. Also both Ross — who was not at his most observant when in company — and Demelza noticed how bitter they were both looking. Nor could it have been anything to do with their own presence, for they had not been seen. Demelza had the impression that they did not speak to each other all night, and this was later confirmed by Caroline, who told her she had heard a rumour that they were on the point of separation.

"Separation?" Demelza said. "But she is going to have another baby!"

Caroline shrugged. "Something has happened this last week or so, I know not what. They were happy enough at my aunt's reception: I saw them laughing together."

"Who did you hear it from?"

"Mrs. Tracey called on them on Tuesday and she said Elizabeth was looking very ill, and that the feeling in the house was most unpleasant.''

''Can it be because of Monk Adderley's death?''

''I would doubt it. I would think it must be something much more personal.''

In the middle of the *soirée* a good-looking man of about forty called Harry Winthrop, who was a relative of the Marquis of Bute, came across and was attentive to Demelza. She was almost rude to him. That evening she came to a decision.

III

It was two days later that Ross saw George in the passageway leading to St. Stephen's Chapel. He was with another member, but there were few other people about. It was now or never. There couldn't be a less unsuitable time to discharge his unpleasant duty.

''George!'' he called, and quickened his pace to catch up; and even as he moved he thought: I should have sent it; I should have sent it round.

George Warleggan turned, and Ross was startled by the look that came on the other's face when he saw who had addressed him. It was a look of such hatred that it stopped Ross in his tracks. If there was purer venom he had never seen it.

Had George cared so much, then, for Monk Adderley?

"Pardon me," George said to his companion. "It seems that I am being solicited in some way. I will rejoin you in a moment."

"Of course." The other man glanced quickly at George's terrible expression and at Ross's slinged arm and the scar on his face. Then he moved on.

"Well?"

Ross said: "As you know, I had a meeting with your friend, Captain Adderley. What occurred at it is not for me to say; but before he died he left a message with me through his friend Mr. John Craven. It is not a message I gladly pass on, since I have no wish to talk to you on the subject, but the last request of a dead man is something I can't ignore."

"Well?" George seemed to have difficulty in speaking at all.

"He commanded me to give you ten guineas." Ross fumbled with his left hand and got the ten pieces out of his fob.

"What — for?"

"I understand he made some wager with you and he lost. I have no idea whether it concerned me, and am not interested to know. I would suppose, since he employed me to do this, that it did. It would fit his sense of the appropriate."

Ross extended the money. George looked at it, then he looked at Ross. The glare in his eyes had not changed.

George put out his hand and Ross gave him the money. George counted it.

Then he flung the ten coins full in Ross's face and turned away.

Perhaps fortunately for all concerned John Bullock, the member for Essex, had just come up to speak to Ross, and he saw the occurrence and was able to grasp him by the arm.

"Steady on, boy, steady on. One quarrel is enough in a session. Let's not have another just yet."

Although nearing seventy, Bullock was a very strong old man, and the grip he had on Ross's arm did not relax.

"You — saw what happened," Ross said, wincing as he moved his bad arm to wipe some spots of blood off his face. "You — saw what happened!"

"Yes, indeed I did. And a sorry waste of good gold it all seemed. If you will permit me I'll pick some of it up for you."

"I could . . ." Ross stopped. He had been going to say "call him out for this," but he realised what Bullock had instantly perceived. Whatever the provocation, a second duel now would finish Ross.

Another member had come up and was picking up the gold, which had rolled in various directions. Both members offered it to Ross, who was now standing in a dazed fashion staring up the long corridor and dabbing at his face. But he refused to accept the coins.

"The money belongs to Warleggan," he said. "I cannot take it. Pray give it to him. I could not trust myself near him at this time."

"I think," said Bullock peaceably, "it had better go in the Poor Box. I fancy not the task of distributing it to either of you."

IV

Ross said nothing to Demelza when he got home, and when she asked him what had bruised his face he said some apprentices had been fighting as he came through the notorious district of Petty France, and that stones had hit him.

A quiet evening, each busy with private thoughts, neither wishing to share them. All the splendid intimacy and happiness of the first week of the London stay was as if it had not been.

Just as she was getting into bed, Demelza said: "Do you feel safe now, Ross?"

"Safe?"

"From the police, I mean. It is three weeks. If they had been going to charge you, would they not have done so by now?"

"I imagine so."

"Caroline was saying so today."

"I'm indebted to her for the reassurance."

"Ross, you must not be sarcastic with me."

"I'm sorry. No, I should not."

"Well I too was 'indebted for the reassurance,' which, it seems, comes not just from Caroline but from St. Andrew St. John, who is a barrister and should know a little as to how the law works. He said he thought the worst risks were over."

"I'm glad."

"*I'm* glad. And your arm is mending?"

"That too." He did not at the time notice her special need of reassurance.

Although they were in bed early Ross slept late. He dreamt horrible dreams of Monk Adderley — that he was a great snake and lay along the floor of the House wriggling and spitting venom. He heard someone screaming, and it was Elizabeth. Then he saw that she and Demelza were going to fight a duel and that he must stand between them to prevent it. And they discharged their shots and showers of coins hit him about the face and head. And then George was saying in a sneering voice: "Thirty pieces of silver. Thirty pieces of silver."

He woke from heavy sleep when it was full day. The curtains were still drawn but the rattle of the carts and the shouting outside told him it must be late. Demelza was already up, for her place was empty.

He raised his head and peered at the clock. Ten minutes past nine.

There was such a row outside that he drew the curtain aside to see what was about. A fight was in progress between two rabbit sellers and some ragged Irish labourers, who had tried to barter some not very fresh and probably stolen fish for the rabbits. That failing, they had tried to help themselves. A crowd of spectators — pedlars, barrow women, servants, apprentices, and all the flotsam of London — had formed round the struggling, cursing men. Whatever the outcome, neither the fish nor the rabbits were going to be saleable after.

Ross pulled the curtain further back and wondered where Demelza was. Then he saw the letter.

It just said:

Ross,
I am going home. Dwight is leaving this morning at seven o'clock from the Crown and Anchor, and I have asked him if I can go with him.

Ross, I do not feel I can stay in London any longer. Whether it be right or wrong I do not know, but I was the cause of the duel between you and Monk Adderley. For aught I know it might happen again. And again.

I should not have come, for I am out of my depth in London society, and my wish to be friendly and polite to everyone was taken to mean something more. It was even taken by you to mean something more.

Ross, I am going home — to your home and your farm and your children. When you return I shall be there, and we can see then what is best to be done.

Love,
Demelza

CHAPTER IX

The hackney chairman said: "What number did ye say, my lady?"

"Fourteen," said Elizabeth.

"Fourteen. That be down at the other hend o' the street, my lady. 'Ave no doubt, Hi'll take ye there."

They jogged down the uneven pavement, thrusting their way among pedestrians with a "By yer leave, sir! By yer leave!"

Pool Lane was a narrow twisting street making its way tortuously northwards from the Oxford Road and growing ever narrower as it proceeded, until, as they reached No. 14, a green door fresh-painted among many that were peeling, Elizabeth almost gave up and told the chairmen to carry her home. Only the memory of the last ten days drove her on.

Since Geoffrey Charles's innocent

remark George had been insufferable. The terrible thing about the observation was that, although not strictly true — Valentine was a boy who seemed to change his appearance like a chameleon with his moods — once made it seemed rather to hang incontrovertibly in the air. It was as if it were a curse rather than a comment. As if the words spoken by Francis's son had been those of a Poldark recognising another Poldark. Something out of the grave. Of course this was wholly untrue — and would have been seen as such in a rational situation. But this was not a rational situation and never had been.

She was even more sick at heart because she saw that under his evil temper George too was sick at heart. Until the moment of Geoffrey Charles's declaration they had been happier together than ever before. Elizabeth was a woman who blossomed in society: though she had had little enough of it in her life, it was her natural element. Years ago when Francis was still alive and she was living a cloistered and poverty-stricken existence at Trenwith, while

Francis gambled away what little money the estate brought in — George had visited her one day and said to her in his deferential voice how much it grieved him to see all her beauty wasted on a few relatives and the empty rooms of a decaying house, when she deserved, and would receive, the acclaim of society if it were ever permitted to see her. He had even ventured to hint that beauty did not last for ever.

Well, all these years later he had been as good as his word. Once before, when he had been member for Truro, she had been up with him for a short time, and that had been pleasant enough; but then he had been unsure of himself, defensive in society, jealous — or at least envious — of the way in which she moved in it as if it were her rightful place. This time had been different. Not only was he assured of his seat for just as long as he cared to occupy it: he owed it to no one but himself, and owed no one allegiance. Indeed, he brought to the Commons the vote of a second member. About a month ago, against his more cautious judgment, he had told Elizabeth of his plans and of the letter he had written under Mr. Robinson's direction to the First Lord of the Treasury, Mr. William Pitt. He had even showed Elizabeth a copy of it, and phrases still echoed in her mind. ". . . that I have settled and composed those matters in the county of Cornwall which in my conversations with Mr. John Robinson I have explained can be used as a means of supporting Government and your Administration. This I shall now uniformly do, as indeed shall be seen henceforth. And such Interests as I may take up will be those which you will call upon me to Support. I wish therefore before Parliament rises to have the honour of an audience at your earliest Conveniency, that closer arrangements may be made . . ."

The "audience" had not yet taken place, but Robinson had assured George that it would, and George had told Elizabeth that while the vulgar notion of a direct *quid pro quo* would not be raised, nevertheless it would be made known to Pitt that a knighthood for Mr. Warleggan would perpetuate the allegiance as no other form of favour was likely to do.

They had both been excited at the thought. To George it would be the accolade both in a literal and in a psychological sense. Once he was Sir George his cup would be full. He might even get a baronetcy in a year or two more, so that the title could be perpetuated. Elizabeth was full of satisfaction at the thought of being Lady Warleggan. Of course her birth assured her more firmly of her position than any mere title. Indeed it had been a tradition in the Chynoweth family — even a proud one — that they had been a line of landowners and distinguished gentlemen for a thousand years with never a title among them. But Elizabeth had been conscious ever since she married George of having lowered herself in the eyes of the county; this would make up.

So she had been convinced that the title if it came, and the new baby when it came, would cement their marriage as nothing before. And she was still beautiful — especially when her hair was done as it had been done at the party on the night of the opening of Parliament. Time might be shorter for her now than that day when George had spoken to her in the winter parlour of Trenwith; but there was still some left.

So everything had been pleasant and satisfactory to contemplate, and one woke in the morning with a good day ahead, one lay in bed before rising, making complicated and agreeable plans for the future.

And in a flash *nothing*. Nothing was satisfactory, *nothing* was pleasant any more. A thoughtless exclamation by her own son had poisoned the very well of their lives. They were back to the situation of three years ago when all the suspicion and distrust had festered and burst into a great quarrel between them. They were back only worse, with more to lose and more already lost. Everything they did now, every breath they drew, was contaminated.

Hence her visit today. One minute she thought herself insane to contemplate it; the next it seemed the only possible way out.

She had paid the chairman, and, with a veil over her face, was greeted by a thin Jewish boy in black silk coat and breeches. She gave her name — Mrs. Tabb — and was ushered in. Three minutes in a waiting room; then she was shown into the room beyond, and Dr. Anselm rose to greet her.

Franz Anselm, born in the ghettoes of Vienna, had arrived in England in 1770, a penniless young man of twenty-two, bringing with him a few guineas stitched into his shirt, and a case of medicines which were confiscated by the excise officers at Dover. He walked to London — as he had walked across Europe — and after a year of near starvation had found employment as a ward assistant in the recently established Westminster Lying-in Hospital. After five years there he had become assistant to a man-midwife called Lazarus, who worked in Cloth Lane, near Golden Square; and when Lazarus unfortunately cut his finger while dissecting a woman who had died of the childbed fever, Anselm came in for the practice. There, with no qualifications, but armed with a tremendous belief in himself, five years of pragmatic observation, an instinct for humanity he had got from his mother, and a copy of William Smellie's *Set of Anatomical Tables,* he had established a reputation.

He had moved to rooms at his present address fifteen years ago, and five years after that had bought the freehold of the house. From the poor women of the city he had made his way to the rich. Although he still had no letters after his name, more and more women came to him, or called him in. They liked him, were impressed by him, often just because he was not as other doctors. He had a new approach, a flexible conscience, an intimate understanding of and tolerance for the ways of the world, and a wide knowledge of continental medicine. Most valuable of all, still, was his mother's instinct for sick people.

At close quarters he looked even more ugly and intimidating then he had done at Mrs. Tracey's reception. His eyes were dewy black sloes peering out from the untrimmed, unkempt hedgerows of immense eyebrows. His upper lip and heavy jowls would not have looked out of place on an ape. The hair of his head might have been judged too woolly, too artificial, if it had been seen on a doll.

"Mrs. — er — Tabb," said Dr. Anselm in a very gentle, attractive voice that surprised coming from so big a man. "Have we met before?"

"No," said Elizabeth. "I have had you recommended to me."

"May I ask by whom?"

"I'd prefer — she'd prefer not to say."

"Very well. How may I be of service to you?"

Elizabeth licked her lips. She found she couldn't begin. He waited a few moments and then lifted his eyebrows.

"Perhaps I may get you something to drink, Mrs. — er — Tabb. A cordial, some orange juice? I don't keep spirits."

"No . . . thank you. What I have to say, Dr. Anselm, is — in the greatest confidence . . . You'll appreciate . . ."

"My dear madam, many titled people, including two duchesses and two princesses, have done me the favour of giving me their confidence. If I could not keep it I could not keep my practice, nor should I wish to."

It was a strange room she was in — too luxuriously furnished for good taste. It was as if Dr. Anselm had compensated not only his body for those thin hard years, but his senses also. The carpet was Arabian, of the most brilliant red and yellow, with an intricate geometric design. The curtains were French: heavily worked silk from Lyon. Tapestries covering the walls were French also, with scenes of the Old Testament. The chair in which she sat was of a luxury hardly met with in the furniture of the day. The chandeliers were Venetian. The only evidence of the use to which the room might sometimes be put was a long flat couch with a coverlet of pale yellow silk. She suppressed a shiver and hoped she might not be asked to lie on it.

"I am thirty-five," she said abruptly. "I married quite young. Then my husband died. I have remarried. Now I am with child."

Dr. Anselm's thick lips parted in a

gentle smile. "So."

"Let me say at once that it is not illegitimate."

"Ah, so . . ."

"Also that I do not wish to lose the baby."

"I'm glad to know that. In any case, Mrs. — er — Tabb, if I observe you correctly, you are now — what — five months forward?"

"Six."

"Good. Good." He nodded his head and waited.

"I'm told," Elizabeth said, "that you have many abilities, Dr. Anselm."

"I have been told so."

"Well, for reasons I can't explain — don't wish to explain — I would like this to be a seven-month or eight-month child."

He looked his surprise and then away. There was a long silence. A French ormolu clock struck the half hour.

"You mean you wish to come to parturition before the appointed time?"

"Yes . . ."

"But you would like the child to

772

be born alive?"

"Yes, yes. Of *course.*"

He put the tips of his hairy fingers together and stared down at the carpet.

"Is it *possible?*" Elizabeth asked at length.

"It is possible. But not easy. And there would be risk."

"To me or to the baby?"

"Either or both."

"How much risk?"

"It would depend. I would have to examine you."

Oh, God, she thought.

"Have you had other children?"

"Yes, two."

"How old were you?"

"My first — when my first was born I was twenty. My second — I would be twenty-nine."

"A considerable interval. Were they by the same man?"

"No."

"And now there is another interval — five and a half — six years?"

"It will be six years to the month if this child comes to its proper term."

"I see. Were there any complications at the birth of your other children?"

"No."

"And they were both full-term?"

She hesitated. ". . . Yes."

"When did you miss your first menses?"

"This time? In May."

"Can you be more specific?"

"It was the fourteenth. I particularly remember. Perhaps the thirteenth."

"Are your showings regular or do they vary in occurrence and length?"

"Regular. Sometimes they vary in length."

The chair creaked as Dr. Anselm reared his great bulk out of it and took his stomach across to a Chinese cupboard. He opened it and took out a calendar and laid it on the Louis Quinze desk. He dipped his pen in an inkwell and scratched some figures on a piece of paper.

"That means that you should come to your full term in February, most likely the early part. What you want me to do is to advise you how you may have your child, alive and well, in December or

January. Am I right?"

"Yes."

"Are you living in London? Would you wish me to attend you?"

"I had intended staying in London, but now I think I shall go back to — well, my house in the country."

Franz Anselm rubbed the feather against his chins, which, although shaved three hours ago, were already dark again.

"Mrs. Tabb. Before I go any further, may I ask you to consider what you are doing. Nature sets out immutable laws and is not lightly to be interfered with. Had you come to me with a two-month pregnancy I could have terminated it far more easily, and more safely, than what you are asking me to do. Indeed, although it is quite possible to do it, and although you look to be in good health, I would remind you that you are thirty-five, which is a disadvantage. Secondly, and more importantly, you would be asking me to prescribe a medicine whose effects I should not be in a position to supervise or oversee."

Elizabeth nodded, wishing she

had never come.

Anselm said: "Indeed, I suppose I am right in assuming that you would wish this to appear a *naturally* premature birth, and that the presence of a doctor openly intending to produce this result would be contrary to your wishes."

She nodded again.

Silence fell in the room, but the bells of the hawkers outside were persistent.

"Sometimes there is little peace even at night," said Dr. Anselm. "The penny post comes at midnight and sets up such a clamour with his bell. Often, too, notices are read late in order to attract more attention. And some of the street men never seem to sleep."

Elizabeth said: "Dr. Anselm, I think I was wrong to come to you. I should not have done so had I not been in great distress."

"Please sit down. I appreciate what you say, madam. We must discuss this coolly and quietly for a little while, and then it may seem easier to decide what is to be done."

She subsided miserably and waited.

He passed across the room and came back with a glass of sweetened fruit juice, which she sipped. He nodded at that approvingly.

"A recipe of my own. Very soothing to the nerves. . . . Mrs. Tabb."

"Yes?"

"What I suggest — what I will suggest to you is that if my examination shows you to be in good health and the pregnancy — so far as I can tell at this stage — a normal one, I will make up a medicine for you, which you may take away with you today. It is a simple vegetable remedy, compounded of a distillation of a number of valuable herbs and of a fungus that grows on rye. If you take it as prescribed — neither more nor less; the amount will be carefully written down for you — and at the date prescribed — you are likely to produce a living child in the manner you desire. I shall put down two dates, one in December and one in January. It will be for you to choose, but I would certainly recommend the December one."

"Why?"

"At seven months the child, though less mature, is suitably positioned for birth. Towards the eighth month it turns and is not so positioned. There are far more children born alive at seven months than eight."

"I see."

"What I suggest is that you take this medicine away with you and keep it always by you. When the time comes you may decide not to take it after all, and then you will go to your full term as nature has designed. But if you are still of the same mind, then it will be available to you as required. I presume you will have a physician to attend you at the time?"

"Oh, yes."

"Good. Ah, so . . . Well, if there should be any complications — if, for instance, uterine spasms continue for long after the birth of the child — do not hesitate to take the doctor into your confidence. You could become ill yourself, and it would then be necessary for him to know what you had taken. After all, I am not the only doctor in the world capable of keeping his own counsel."

Elizabeth gave him a wan smile.

"However, that need not be and should not be. The fine blending of these herbs should prevent such complications."

"Thank you."

"Very well, then," said Dr. Anselm. "If you would kindly lie on this couch. I shall confine my examination to the mere essentials, so that it may be as little distressing to you as possible."

CHAPTER X

Demelza's long journey home with Dwight was one in which she was torn between a feeling that she had deserted Ross in what might yet be a crisis, and a stronger conviction that she could stay no longer with him in London. An impossible situation had been reached, and the only way was to separate. Whatever effect this might have on their future together, it could be no worse than the risk that would otherwise be run.

As they neared home, she tried to put aside all the bitterness and the heartache of a London visit which had promised and begun so well. However Ross felt when he returned — whatever was going to happen to their marriage — just now, within a day, within a few hours, within a few minutes, she was going to be reunited with her children and her home and her friends and servants and everything — except Ross — that she cared most about in the world. She must concentrate her thoughts on that.

It was strange coming back to Cornwall after her first time away. She saw again its barrenness, but also she instantly breathed in the soft air like a tonic. She understood the county's overall indigence and untidiness compared to the well-groomed and wealthy countryside through which she had passed. She felt once again that there was not the enormous gap in Cornwall between rich and poor. The great houses, with one or two exceptions, were much smaller than up-country, and there were many fewer. The poor in Cornwall, so far as she could judge, were no poorer, the gentry more on terms with their work people.

The only way from Truro was to hire horses, and this they did. She wanted Dwight to fork off for Killewarren, but he insisted on seeing her home. So she came, and suddenly there was great commotion and squeals of delight, and her hat was knocked away and a pair of fat and a pair of thin arms were round her, and Jane and John Gimlett were crowding in and Betsy Maria Martin and Ena Daniel and all the rest. Presently Clowance burst into noisy tears, and when asked why, replied it was because Mama was crying. Demelza said, what nonsense, she never cried, it was because she had an onion in her pocket; but when they clamoured to see it she could only produce an orange. When Dwight turned to go she asked him to stay the night, knowing that no child waited to welcome him, but he shook his head and said he was anxious to see Clotworthy.

Over the next day talk never stopped at Nampara. The children were well, although Jeremy had been at death's door with a boil on his arm. At least this was what Jeremy said, but it happened to be his favourite phrase at the moment. He had heard Mr. Zacky Martin use it, and liked it so much that he brought it in whenever possible. Clowance had actually *grown,* though without any sign yet of shedding her puppy fat. Neither of the children, Demelza thought, looked as *clean* as they ought. Although they had probably had more attention than when she was at home, they looked a little neglected and untidy. It was very strange. They lacked the lick of the mother cat.

Also things had not been so good among the servants while she was away. When she was at home complete tranquillity reigned. Now it seemed that Mrs. Kemp had presumed too much (or done not enough), that Jane Gimlett had found Betsy Maria Martin disobedient (or had been too harsh with her), that John Gimlett had not told Jack Cobbledick something about the pigs that he should have done (or had to do something Cobbledick had neglected). And so backwards and forwards in respectful, or not so respectful, asides, until Demelza told each one privately that she wished to hear no more, that she was glad to be home, and that henceforward everything must return to its previous harmony.

All this should have helped her put events in London out of mind, or at least into the background. Instead contact with all the familiar things, all the preoccupations of a busy family life, accentuated her awareness of every detail of her stay in London, as a bright light will accentuate shadows. Production at the mine, as Zacky had written them, was up for the month of October and he now reported it up for November too. At the coinage in Truro their stuff had sold well, and prices generally had risen. Wheal Maiden was still barren of tin, but a modest amount of red copper, not dissimilar from that mined in the recently extinct Wheal Leisure, was now being brought up, also small quantities of silver and silver-lead. These last were never likely to be found in such amounts as to justify the outlay of working a mine to bring them up, but as a by-product they were a small addition to the profit side of the ledger.

On the second day Sam called. He kissed his sister, an act which she always felt he performed with a proper mixture of respect and religious circumstance. She was his elder sister, and the wife of the squire; but she was also his daughter in

Christ. She asked at once about Drake.

He said: "He's back in Pally's Shop, as your — as Ross instructed him — and working. The roof is repaired, the outside washed, some furniture bought and made, and what ye kindly sent by way of curtains, carpets, and mats have been put to the best use. His trade be back — that which he lost, I mean — and his fields are soon to be ploughed. But he have not yet climbed out of the mire of despond into which his spirit and his soul have fallen. I fear that the pains of hell have got hold upon him and that he is yet estranged from God."

"Sam," Demelza said; "as I have mentioned before my concern for Drake is not quite the same as yours. Of course I want him to be happy in the next world. But just now I am concerned with his happiness in this. I ask about his *spirits,* not his spirit."

"Sister," Sam said, "Drake is dull and quiet — and that is not his nature, as you well d'know."

"Is he seeing anything of Rosina?"

"Not's I know. I would reckon

nothin 'tall.''

Demelza got up and pushed a lock of hair away from her face. Sam looked at her in her cream dimity frock, with the keys dangling at the waist, and thought how young she still looked. But pale. And less pretty. As if something were dragging at her spirit.

He said: "Is something wrong wi' *your* life, sister? Are ye troubled of body or soul?''

She smiled. "A little perhaps of both, Sam. But it is something I cannot talk about.''

"'Tis easeful always for the soul to unburden itself to Christ.''

"And that I cannot do neither. Though maybe more's the pity . . . But tell me of Drake. Did he ever say — did he never tell you what happened when he went to Truro?''

"Mrs. Whitworth would not see him. She turned him away as if they was strangers. Drake said she had changed so's ye would not know her. Almost crazed she was, he says. And of course looking on Drake as far beneath her now. Ah, well . . . Twould have been a bad marriage whether or no, but Drake could not see that until it were too late. . . . Did I ever tell you two constables called? . . ."

"When? On you? What about?"

Demelza listened to Sam's story with a gathering coldness in her heart, half attending to the monstrous suspicion implied by the visit, half thinking of Ross and wondering whether someone might yet call on *him*. If they did, and she were not there, what might he not be trapped into admitting? Her stomach turned over within her. Certain that if the Cornish law had taken the trouble to stretch out its fingers and touch Drake, then the London law, which must be so much more efficient and so much more severe, could hardly fail to move against Ross in the end. . . .

"So I've wondered oft, if Lady Whitworth thought such a thing . . ."

With difficulty she brought her attention fully back to Sam. "What do you mean?"

"Well, Mrs. Whitworth — Morwenna — she did claim to be in love wi' Drake.

That she should reject him just like that — so sharp, so unfriendly — I've thought since, if Lady Whitworth thought Drake .might've had a hand in Mr. Whitworth's death, Morwenna might've thought the same."

"D'you mean that being why she turned him away?"

"Mebbe."

Demelza thought, and then shook her head conclusively.

"Whatever else, Morwenna, if she cared at all for Drake, must have come to know him well. No one who ever comes to know Drake well could ever suspect him of such a thing."

They moved on a few paces. How long now before Ross left London? Perhaps only a few days. Perhaps he had already left — if he was permitted to . . . What, she wondered, would her leaving him imply to him when he read her note? Their relationship at this moment seemed the most impossible of resolution that had ever been. Everything they did, said, thought, took place behind endless barriers of hurt pride and misunderstanding.

"What did you say, Sam? I'm sorry."

"I just wondered — when you've been Tehidy — I wondered if maybe you'd ever seen Emma?"

"I've not been to Tehidy while she's been there. Ross has been two or three times, but then he hardly knew her. Do you want me to ask?"

Sam squeezed his knuckles. "Nay. She's wed, and I pray she will be happy wed. Tis best left at that."

Demelza said bitterly: "There's a saying in London that hell is paved with good intentions. That seems to be what happens to all my good intentions, both for my brothers and for myself."

Sam put a hand on her arm. "Never say that, sister. Never regret anything you do out of the goodness of your heart."

II

Two days later she walked the five miles to see Drake, feeling that life in London had been too sedentary, and that anyway perhaps the exercise would help to calm some of the crosscurrents in her heart.

Also they said Jud Paynter was very ill, so she could call on him on the way. She didn't want anyone *else* to die.

Up the nutty valley with the red stream bubbling beside her and Wheal Grace smoking; the clang of stamps, the braying of donkeys, the rattle of carts (was London after all that much noisier?), past Wheal Maiden, down towards Sawle Church, past the tract leading to Sawle Combe. Goats were pasturing on the bare moorland, living comfortably on what no other domestic animal could subsist on. (She should really also call at the Nanfans', for Char had been ill.)

When she got to the Paynters' she was relieved to see Jud sitting up in bed and looking little different. Thinner, certainly — like a bulldog that had been pickled in spirit — but as full of complaints as ever and eating all that was put before him. Prudie admitted that he had been some slight, but then, she said, twas only gouty wind and bile, and it all came from him getting drunk last Wednesday sennight at Tweedy's kiddley, and then mistooken the road home and fallen into Parker's timber pond, and twas a pity he hadn't drownded there and then so he could have put an end on it.

Timber ponds were pools, or parts of a dammed stream, where wood was seasoned before use. The timber lying in them was very greasy, and Jud bitterly commented on the fact.

"I were feeling nashed afore ever this, I tell ee! Nay, Missus, twas naught to do wi' drink. *Sober* I were and walking home as slow as a dew snail. Hat on head, nose warmer in mouth, I were quaddling home as slow as a dew snail all along of me feeling slight from all the work I done that day teeling in widow Treamble. Gurt woman, she were, and her coffin, twas all we could do to prize un into the 'ole. They d'say she wouldn't go in the coffin proper way round so they 'ad to thrust 'er in backsyfore. And that's 'ow she'll *stay,* backsyfore till the Day of Judgment! And who d'know what the Lord God will say when He see a woman edging out of 'er coffin backsyfore? Shocked He'll be, I reckon, shamed, He'll be at such a sight! . . . Shouldn't wonder if the same thing don't 'appen to you, Prudie, when it come your turn.''

"Twill not be afore I've seen *you* closed 'ome,'' said Prudie.

"Well, yur were I, Missus, walking 'ome, sober as a judge, or maybe soberer, and I come to this yur bridge — twas no more'n ten paces acrost — and I started acrost 'n, and by ivers, soon's I put foot 'pon the planchin, then the planchin began to give way! An' it slid, an' it slid, an' it slid, like you was on a frosty road covered wi' goose turds. Step I took, one 'pon t'other, each one rolling and slipping fasterer than the last un, till at last me feet flew from under me and plosh! I were in the water. Deep, deep, I sank, and a-swallowin' of un, and tasting like a drang. Twas a mercy I were brave 'nough to find me way 'ome! An I never been right since!''

"Never was right afore,'' said Prudie. "Nor never will be. Not till kingdom come. Nor after that. Long after that. When the sun d'grow cold Jud Paynter'll still not be right. 'Cos you wasn't *born* right, see!''

Demelza stayed for twenty minutes, hearing the gossip of the countryside, and then escaped into the more wholesome air outside and, when Prudie followed her, gave her her usual half guinea. Prudie was pathetically grateful, but long before Demelza was out of earshot she heard the rumble of argument begin again inside the cottage.

Through Grambler and past the gates of Trenwith, and the detour that everyone now accepted to avoid trespassing on Warleggan land. So towards Trevaunance Cove and Place House just out of sight over the headland. Here some oxen were being used to plough a field and she could hear the small boys who were driving them keep up a rhythmic chant of encouragement. *"Come* on, Fallow, *come* on, Chestnut. *Now,* then, Tartar, *now* then, County. *Come* on, Fallow, *come* on Chestnut, *now* then, Tartar, *now* then, County." So the singsong drawl went on. She stood to watch them for a time. A ridge of cloud like a woollen blanket hung over the sea.

So down the hill to Pally's Shop.

Drake was shoeing a horse while the farmer waited. He gave her a quick smile and the farmer touched his hat.

"I'll not be long."

"Don't hurry," she said, and passed into the house.

III

They had taken tea and talked long and she was ready to go. He had said more to her than to anyone before; partly because she was his beloved sister whom he had not seen for two and a half months; partly because his last, and final, tragedy was now seven months old. Sick at heart with her own recent memories, she listened to his with the more sympathy.

"I shall never marry now," he said, "any more'n I believe Sam will. It is — over. I feel little of naught now. Like that time before, I work. And work and work. One day it seem me I shall be rich!" He laughed. "Maybe it is a good thing if you d'want to make money, to be crossed in love. You've little else to think on."

"*You* don't think about making money."

"No, I don't *think* about it: I just work and it come!"

"Drake, you remember the Christmas party of last year? Well, this year Caroline wants to have it there — at Killewarren, instead of Nampara. But otherwise just the same. If she does have it — and we go — I want you to promise to come as you did before."

"*If* you go?"

"Well . . . it will depend. After London it will depend. I do not know how Ross will feel about a Christmas party . . ."

Drake looked at the expression on his sister's face and perceived the depth of the issues that waited for Ross's return.

Demelza said: "But even if we should not be there, Ross and I, or only one of us, I would still wish for you to go. I know Caroline will invite you and Sam. You must not feel any barrier between you because they are rich. They are my dearest friends."

"She've been very good to me. Any work she can she send over here. And

795

sometimes when she was living down here permanent she used to come herself and chat and talk, just like we were equals."

"Well, then."

"Let us wait Christmas, sister."

She looked out at the day. The blanket of cloud had by now drawn itself over the land, putting the sky to bed. "I must go. I told them not to wait dinner for me."

"There's rain in the wind. Stay and eat wi' me."

"Not today, Drake. But thank you."

"I'll come partway home — "

"No, you'll lose custom . . ."

"Custom can wait."

So he walked back with her as far as the top of Sawle Combe. By now misty-wet had set in, and he watched her striding away into the damp grey afternoon, cloak over head, long grey skirt, sturdy shoes, until she was lost to sight among the pines of Wheal Maiden. Then he turned and walked home, bending his head into the gentle soaking rain.

When he reached home farmer Hancock was waiting for him, looking impatient. He had brought two oxen to be shod, and had sent a boy down this morning to tell Drake as much, and Drake had forgot. So the next hour was busy, and when Hancock had gone Drake cut himself a couple of slices from the ham he had bought from the Trevethans yesterday when they killed their pig. This, with bread and tea and two apples, made a good meal, and as soon as it was done another commission kept him busy still four.

So the days went. By now dark was not far off, and the two Trewinnard boys came in from working in his fields, soaked to the skin and anxious to be off home. He let them go, and walked to the gate of his yard to see them scuttling up the hill towards St. Ann's.

Work was less in the winter; few customers came after dark, and the long evenings which he had earlier spent by candlelight making spades and ladders and other things to sell to the mines, he now, since the fire, devoted to building furniture to replace the stuff that had been burned. This he found much more exacting, but it was one of the few things to give him a wholesome sense of satisfaction when done. To begin with he had used inferior wood, but recently he had bought some good oak and walnut, and he was resolved to make over again all the earlier pieces knocked together for quick convenience.

Well, it would not do to stand here endlessly with the wet dripping off his face. No one else was coming now. He had chickens to feed, and some geese he was fattening for Christmas.

He turned away from the gate, and then his sharp eye detected a man in a long coat coming down the hill from St. Ann's carrying a bag. He seemed hesitant, not quite sure where he was going, and sure enough Drake saw him stop at a cottage — the Robertses' — and, it seemed, ask the way. Mrs. Roberts was pointing down the hill. The man came on. He was not smartly dressed but he looked too respectable to be a vagrant or a beggar.

Drake went into the storehouse to get some meal for the chickens. He put it in a bowl to be able to throw it more easily, and fed a few of the chickens, watching them scuttle towards him on long rangy legs and then dart about the yard like thrown knives to jab at the food he scattered.

He heard the click of the gate and went out again. The figure at it said:

"Would you be so kind as to tell me . . . oh," and then in the smallest voice, "Drake!"

Drake dropped the bowl, which rolled on its rim into a corner, spilling the rest of the meal everywhere.

"Oh, my love. . ." he said. "Have you come home?"

IV

She sat opposite him in the tiny parlour, hair still lank from the rain, the lashes of her shortsighted eyes linked with tears. She had dropped her cloak, and sat there in her brown woollen dress like some tall damp bird that had come in for shelter but when it had dried and rested would take flight again. He had knelt to unbutton her black, blunt-toed wet shoes, but she had shrunk from his touch. She was holding a cup of tea, warming her hands with it and trying not to shiver.

"I left this morning . . ." she said, speaking rapidly, without pauses. "Early this morning; I thought at first I thought I should leave her a note; but that seemed — cowardly; I felt that, if I have sometimes been cowardly in the past, now was the time to stop; so I went into her bedroom before she was up and told her what I was going to do. At first she laughed — did not believe me — then when she saw I really intended she grew . . . swollen with rage; it was something — something my — something Osborne used to be able to do . . . to grow bigger in anger, in annoyance, in — in frustration."

He watched her in silence, hardly able yet to believe she was here.

"She said she would have me stopped; she said she would call the servants, get me locked up — then have me put away, she said, as Osborne had once tried to have me put away; I said she had no right — no one had any right — I was a widow now; anyway, what did she care, I asked her, about me? What did she care? I was only an expense and a nuisance; I was going to leave her my son . . . my son.''

''Don't talk, Morwenna, if it upset you.''

''I *want* to talk, Drake; I *must* talk. I must tell you everything I *can* . . .''

At that point she choked and was quiet for a while. The hot tea was burning colour in her cheeks.

''So when she had shouted at me for — for a long time, then she said, all right, I could go, but if I went, she said, I must take only what I stood up in, and if I went I must never come crawling back; I said I would go and never come back, I said . . . crawling or any other way. So then I left and walked to a farm nearby, and the farmer gave me a lift in his cart to Grampound, and there, after waiting hours, I caught the stage to Truro; then I had to wait again until I found a wagon coming this way; it came as far as Goonbell, and then — I walked from there; I had to ask often because I had really no idea — where you lived.''

He stared at her and stared at her. The last time he had seen her close to like this, personally, in quiet conversation, was more than four years ago. He was recognising her all over afresh. Eventually she looked up at him and he looked away.

"You've eaten?"

"This morning."

"I've got some ham. And there's a morsel of cheese. And there's apples. Bread."

She shook her head, as if dismissing an irrelevancy.

He said: "Let me get ee a blanket to wrap yourself with."

She said: "Drake, I have to tell you about April."

"Does it matter now?"

"It does to me. I have to tell you. Even if it hurts you to tell you."

"Go on then. I mind for nothing of that, though."

She picked some strands of damp hair off her brow. Her eyes were like pools lying in shadow.

"You know I never cared for Osborne?"

"You hated him."

She considered this. "D'you know,

when I was young I didn't know what hate was? I never — it never entered my being. Only after I was married. It's a terrible thing. It shrivels up all that's good in you. It's like a child becoming an old woman in a few months." She shivered. "I'd like to forget I ever felt that for *him* — or for any man. Drake, can I just say I never *cared* for Osborne?"

"So be it."

"After John — my baby — was born I was ill, and I was more ill and sick in spirit when I found that Osborne, while I was ill, had taken another woman; I cannot tell you who it was, but to me it was so physically degrading — so degrading — not that I ever wanted him *back!* . . . Oh, I am telling this so very badly!"

He got up and took the cup from her, refilled it and gave it back to her. He noticed again how she seemed to shrink at his touch.

"Then after some months — I can't recollect how many months — this other woman, she left, and he wanted to resume his relationship with me. I refused — and we had vile quarrels. I continued to refuse him, and made terrible threats. For a long time — I think it must have been two years, I did not let him touch me. . . . But then, only about six weeks before he died it — came about . . . well, he forced himself on me. And after that. Not just once, you see. When it had begun, it happened again and again . . ."

He clenched his fists. "Do you have to tell me this?"

"*Yes!* For I have to explain that when he died I felt *contaminated* — as if the mere thought of the contact between flesh and flesh — any flesh — would turn me sick and demented. Sometimes earlier when I had denied him he had called me demented — but I was far nearer to that just after he had died, after he had died, than at any other time in my life! Do you understand it *at all,* Drake? All that was — was beautiful between us, all that was tender, all that was true — all that perhaps there might be between any young man and any young woman — though I can scarce believe many felt it so deep as we did — all, *all* that was turned to ugliness, beastliness, vileness . . ."

She put the teacup down on the table, her hand not too certain. The fire Drake had lit was crackling with new wood, and the hem of her skirt was drying.

She said: "When I was about fifteen I went with my father once to St. Neot, where he was preaching. On the way home on the following day we happened upon a stag hunt, and I saw a young deer killed . . . I shall never forget it. Suddenly all its grace and its lissom beauty were stretched on a rock, and a knife came and slit open its belly, and all its entrails, its heart, its liver, its bowels, were pulled out to steam and stink in the sun!"

"Morwenna!"

"But it was the *same* deer, Drake, the *same* deer! And when you came I could see only the physical contact of two bodies which would turn my mind to the deepest revulsion, my flesh to shrivel and creep, my stomach to retch. So you see I was — a little — still am a little — demented."

"My love — "

"Also," she said. "I found — I knew that week that he died — that I was with child by him again."

"Then? . . ." He looked at her, instinctively glanced at her waist.

"I lost it two months ago. Oh, not deliberate. I did nothing. But I think perhaps the poor little thing knew that I . . . hated it. That word! I said I'd not use it again. I lost the baby. It just happened."

He breathed out slowly. "And so — now you have come."

"Now I felt I could at least come to see you."

"More'n *that,* I pray. Where else can you go?"

"To Trenwith."

He did not speak but went to the fire to stir it again, crouched there, then went swiftly down the two steps to the kitchen, cut a piece of bread and sliced some ham thinly upon it, brought it on a plate. "Eat this."

"I don't want it."

"Ye *need* it. Must need it after so long a fast."

Reluctantly she bit a corner, chewed, and swallowed, bit again. He watched her. When she had done she half smiled at him.

"Why Trenwith?" he asked.

"It is the best place to go. My cousin's father and mother live there."

"Do you want to see them special?"

"They were always kind."

"But you came here first."

"I had to see you — to explain."

"Is that all?"

"Yes . . . that's all."

A long silence fell between them.

Drake said: "When I came Truro to see ye, I thought to bring you away, to ask you to marry me so soon as ever twas decent after his death. I was — in such a hurry — an impulse — I should've know better."

"You were not to know what I have told you."

"But now . . . Will you marry me, Morwenna?"

She shook her head, not looking at him. "I can't, Drake."

"Why not?"

"Because of what I've told you. Because I feel as I do feel."

"What do that mean?"

"There's so little I can give you."

"You can give me yourself. That's all I want."

"That's just what I can't *do.*"

"Why not my love?"

"Drake, you haven't understood. Because I am still — contaminated — in my mind. I can't look on — on love — on what marriage means — without *revulsion.* If you were to kiss me now I might not shiver, for other people have kissed me. It could be just a salute. But if you were to touch my body I would shrink away because instantly across my mind would come the thought of *his* hands. Did you notice when you tried to unbutton my shoes?"

"Yes."

"Well, shoes particularly I could not — not stand. But *everything.* Because I *am* demented. A little. In that respect. The thought of — of lying with a man — the bodily contact — and what follows it . . . the — the very thought! . . ." She put her head down.

"Even with me?"

"Even with you . . ."

She took her glasses out of her bag and rubbed them on a handkerchief. "I had to take them off when I was walking here because the fine rain blinded me. Now I can see you better. Drake," she said in a matter-of-fact voice. "I must go. Thank you for — for welcoming me. After the way I treated you in April, you are so good, so kind."

He stood up, but not over her, keeping his distance. "Morwenna, I must tell you that just before he — Mr. Whitworth — died I had engaged to marry a girl in Sawle called Rosina Hoblyn. I'd thought that you were lost to me for ever. Kind friends thought my life was being wasted, lost. So twas. So I engaged to marry Rosina. But when I heard *he* was dead, I went see Rosina and asked her to set me free. This she did, for she's a straight, honest, good girl. And I came Truro. And you turned me away. But when you turned me away I didn't go back to Rosina — even if she'd have had me. I resolved never to marry 'tall. I told my sister — she was over today — I told her only

809

today that I should never marry 'tall. And that is the honest truth, without a word of a lie! So . . ." He looked down at her.

"So?"

"Would it not be better to marry me than to see me have no wife — all my days?"

She put her free hand hard to her mouth. "Drake, you still don't *understand.*"

"Oh, yes, I reckon I do." He moved to sit on his haunches in front of her, but checked himself in time. He crouched some way away. "Be my wife in name — marry me — in church proper — that's all I ask. Love — what you call love — carnal love — if it d'come some day it come. If not, not. I shall not press. Twill be for you always to say."

She released her mouth long enough to say: "I couldn't *ask* it. It wouldn't be fair on you. You *love* me! I know that. So how could you — how could you keep a promise it wouldn't be fair to ask you to make?"

"When I make a promise I make it. Don't you love me enough to believe that?"

She shook her head.

"Look," she said, "Why have you come here today?"

She stared at him.

He said patiently: "Was it not because ye wanted to see me?"

She nodded.

He said: "There's more to life than carnal love, isn't there?"

"Yes . . . oh, yes, but — "

"Be honest. Do you not really want to be with me? With me more than anyone else in the world."

She hesitated a long moment, then nodded again.

"But — "

"Then be that not the most important thing of all? Being together. Working together. Talking together. Walking together. There's so *much* to love — even if it be not the love you mean. The sunrise, and the rain and the wind and the cloud, and the roaring of the sea and the cry of birds and the — the lowing of cows and the glow of corn and the smells of spring. And food and fresh water. New-laid eggs, warm milk, fresh-dug potatoes, home-made jams.

Wood smoke, a baby robin, bluebells, a warm fire . . . I could go on and on and on. But if you enjoy them wi' the one you love, then it is enjoyment *fourfold!* D'you think I would not give all my life to see ye sitting in that chair? What is life if you live it alone?"

"Oh, Drake," she said, tears suddenly running down her face and over the hand across her mouth and onto the other hand. They splashed onto her frock where it was already wet with the rain. "Oh, dear — I was — I was — afraid of this . . ."

"Ye cann't be afraid of having what you most want in life."

"No . . . Afraid of my own weakness. Afraid I should never convince you. I love you, of course. I have said it so often to myself in the night. Often it has been like an anthem — giving me strength. But that doesn't mean I am a whole woman any longer. Drake, I am — damaged — and crippled . . . inside . . . in my *mind!*"

"There now," he said. "See, I'm not going to come nigh you, not even to wipe away your tears."

CHAPTER XI

Parliament adjourned on the twentieth of November, and was not to reassemble until the twenty-first of January. Those members who returned for the next session would come back into a new life, a new century.

With two months to kill, the Warleggans decided to return to Cornwall after all. Elizabeth was set on it now, and George made no objection. At the moment he seemed to have little interest in her, or the disputed child who travelled with them. Nor did he seem to care much about the child she now so obviously bore. Although their return was not hurried, there was none of the leisurely, triumphant progress of the journey up. If the coach jogged her it jogged her; if the length of the stages tired her they tired her; if the bedrooms were draughty they were draughty. They reached Truro on Sunday the first of December, but there was so much sickness in the town that Elizabeth said she would prefer to move to Trenwith. George said she must do as she pleased, he had business to attend to. (He had indeed, for some of the tenants at St. Michael were being obstinate and refusing to move.) Elizabeth drove to Trenwith on the fifth, taking Valentine with her.

Ross saw Caroline on the twenty-first, and she said, could he wait a few days for her and they would travel down together? Her maid would be with her, she pointed out, so they would be fully chaperoned, unlike *his* wife and *her* husband. Ross had been helping John Craven tidy up Monk Adderley's estate and to settle up some of the debts he had left, so he agreed. If he were yet to be visited and questioned, well, it would happen — another day or two would not make the difference — he had become fatalistic about it. But as each day followed the other there was still no summons, no knock upon the door from anyone representing the Crown. Once he called on Andromeda Page, but she had already taken up with a young earl recently down from Cambridge and had little time to waste on a lost lover. Thus passes away the glory of the world . . .

On Saturday the thirtieth of November on the same coach, departing from the Crown and Anchor in the Strand at seven o'clock in the morning, Ross and Caroline and her maid left for Cornwall. In spite of the pretence to the contrary that he kept up even with himself, he was glad to be away. . . . When he came back, *if* he came back, the thing would be too far in the past.

On the sixth of December Demelza received a message delivered by one of the Trewinnard twins, and she at once rode to Pally's Shop. Drake met her at the gate. His face told her everything.

"Is she? . . ."

"Inside. I said I'd asked ee to come."

As he helped her off her horse he held her hand a moment longer than necessary. "Sister . . . treat her kind."

Demelza smiled. "Do you think I should not do?"

"No . . . That's why I sent. But I think — "

"Think what?"

"That if anything goes amiss she'll just flee again. Just go . . ."

Morwenna was in the upper room peeling potatoes. She stood up at once and took off her glasses. Demelza smiled at her and she half smiled back and smoothed down her apron, looking tall and uncertain and out of place.

"Mrs. Poldark . . ."

"Mrs. Whitworth."

"Please — sit down."

"I think," Demelza said, "it would be better if we used our first names."

They sat down, Morwenna employing the bowl and the knife and the basket almost as a line of defence.

Demelza looked round the shabby little room. After a moment she said: "Drake badly needs someone to look after him."

"Yes . . ."

"He says he wants you to look after him."

"Yes."

"Do you want that, Morwenna?"

"I think so . . . It is just that I don't know if I am fit."

"Are you ill?"

"Oh, no. I'm strong. Physically I'm strong."

"Then? . . ."

Drake came in with the inevitable tea and for a few minutes they sat drinking it and not talking much. Then Drake, with considerable tact, edged Morwenna round to repeating some of the conversation that had passed last night.

At the end of it Demelza said quietly: "Drake has been very miserable, Morwenna, ever since you left — all these years. He's only been half a person. Now you have come back to him, do you not think it a pity to separate again?"

"Yes . . . But — "

"You have told him how you feel about marriage, and he fully accepts that if you marry him now his marriage shall not be a full one — unless you should ever change. He swears he will respect your wishes."

"Yes, he does."

"Do you believe him?"

Morwenna looked at Drake.

"Yes . . ."

"So will you marry him?"

Morwenna looked round the room, her eyes half seeking some escape. At length she licked her lips and said: "I know I only want to be with him for the rest of my life . . ."

"I don't think," Demelza said, "that there can be a much better reason for marriage than that."

Morwenna said desperately: "So long as he *understands*. I'm not *normal* any longer. I'm not! I'm not!"

Drake said to Demelza: "I explained to her last night. Just being with her is better'n anything else that could be."

Demelza said: "You'll excuse me for mentioning this, but being a blacksmith's wife is that different from being a vicar's wife. There's no social position, like, and there may be work — hard work with hands. Drake could not afford to keep a servant. You *have* thought on that?"

"That!" said Morwenna contemptuously. "I was the eldest of a family of girls. And my mother was never strong. I was the strong one. So I learned to cook and to look after a house. Of course we had servants, but they didn't do all . . . These last years I've lived the life of a lady — cooked for, waited on, treated as a person of importance. So little have I had physically to work. But in my mind and soul I have envied the tween maid, the gardener's daughter, the beggar at the door; I would rather have swept the streets than been in my position! Do you think I would not work now?"

"To be with Drake?"

She hesitated again. "Yes."

"You could wash his clothes — scrub his floors?"

"No need for that," said Drake.

"Of *course*," said Morwenna. "It's nothing — nothing."

Demelza nodded. "And you will not mind if your mother is upset?"

"I'm near twenty-five," said Morwenna harshly. "It is not anything any relative would say that would make the difference."

So young, Demelza thought, and glanced from one to the other. Morwenna looked much older than that, much older than Drake. That was what suffering did. But who knew what happiness might do? Demelza had been against this match almost from the first. Not an personal grounds but on the grounds of Morwenna's unsuitability, her genteel upbringing, her connection with the Warleggans. Yet . . . Drake's eyes. A difference here from yesterday.

"So you'll marry him, Morwenna?"

"I thought I had answered."

"Not yes."

"Then . . . yes."

It had taken a time to reach this word, as if Morwenna had had to plough through fields of reservations and restraints to reach it. Drake stirred and let out a low breath.

Demelza said: "I'm that glad for you both."

"How soon can we be wed?" Drake asked.

"It will take a while. Morwenna, why do you not come and stay with us at Nampara? We should be happy to have you."

"I'd better prefer she stayed

here," said Drake.

Demelza smiled. "It's for Morwenna to say. If you are going to go on living in this district, maybe you should consider what people will say."

"I don't care," Morwenna said.

"I can get Mrs. Trewinnard to come in and sleep," said Drake. If need be I can sleep in the Trewinnards' cottage."

"Whatever you say, Drake," Morwenna said.

"It *should* be Morwenna's decision," Demelza insisted.

Morwenna hesitated. "I'm sorry. Sometimes I have difficulty in concentrating. . . . I'll stay, Demelza. Thank you. I'll stay here."

Demelza kissed her. "When you *are* married, and Drake knows you're safe caught, then I hope he'll bring you to Nampara and you can meet Ross — properly and to get to know — and we can have — other happy times together."

She went out. After a moment Drake came after her and laid his cheek against hers.

"Bless you, sister. Bless you, and can ye do something more this morning?"

"What is that?"

"Come with me to Parson Odgers. Tis some awful to think we must wait three weeks! Is there no way to cut the waiting short?"

"Does it matter?"

"I'm scared for her," he said. "It's just the way you said — safe caught. She's *not* yet safe caught — not till we're wed. I'm scared something may happen. I'm scared she may just change her mind and move on."

II

Mr. Odgers said: "Well, Mrs. Poldark, ma'am, I would be happy to oblige you if there were a way within the canon laws of the church, but as you know, ma'am, there is none. It is Friday now. In order to convenience you I can call the banns for the first time on Sunday, though strictly speaking one needs more notice. But beyond that . . ."

The little clergyman had been flushed

from the kitchen where he had been helping his wife salt a piece of pork. His manner was ingratiating but his feelings mixed. In fact he was deeply shocked. Being a fair man, he would if pressed have been willing to admit that it did not amount exactly to blasphemy that this dean's daughter, the relict of his ex-vicar, on whom he had been accustomed to lavish all the courtesy and deference her station deserved, should now be about to throw the whole of her position away and marry a common smith, and a dissenter at that, but in his view it came very near.

Had that been all, Drake's welcome would have been of the coldest. However, that was not all. Accompanying him was Captain Poldark's wife, and Captain Poldark was a member of Parliament with the "ear" of Viscount Falmouth, and now that the living had again, unexpectedly, even providentially, become vacant, there was still just one more chance, one very last chance, that it might be offered to Mr. Odgers. So he could not afford to offend in the smallest way Captain Poldark's wife.

Captain Poldark's wife wrinkled her brows and said: "Isn't there something, Mr. Odgers, I've heard about or read about called a special licence?"

"Ah, yes, ma'am. That is only obtainable from the Archbishop of Canterbury. But a licence, ma'am, a licence as distinct from a special licence, can be obtained from the Archdeacon of Cornwall, or from his representative, his officer in the county."

"And who would that be?"

Mr. Odgers scratched under his horsehair wig. "The Archdeacon normally, I believe, lives in Exeter, except when he is on one of his — er — visitations. But his court is in Bodmin. I believe if you were to go there, if the young man were to go there" — he couldn't bear to address him by name — "and someone were to go with him to swear a bond, then, I believe, ma'am, a licence might be granted, and then I could perform the wedding soon after receiving it."

Demelza looked at Drake. "That would be about five and twenty miles. Fifty there and back. Would you wish to go so far?"

Drake nodded.

"What do you have to do?" she asked.

"You would have to swear an affidavit that there are no lawful impediments. Or *he* would, ma'am. And take a witness that he is resident in this parish. He *is* in this parish, is he? Yes, just." Mr. Odgers admitted this resentfully. "He would need money. I think it is two guineas, but I am not sure. And the person accompanying him would have to be prepared to be jointly bonded with him in some considerable sum."

"Can a woman act in such a way?"

"Oh, yes. But not his — not his intended. . ."

"I was thinking of myself."

"Mind," said Mr. Odgers, "you had best wait till Monday, to make sure of finding him in. The clergyman, I mean, who acts as the archdeacon's surrogate. Weekends and Sundays are busy times, and he might be away."

Outside again in the windy morning Demelza said: "Well, that's the best we can do."

"You'd lend me a horse?"

"Oh, yes."

"And come yourself?"

"I think. I'd be better than Sam. Being married to Ross gives me a sort of . . ."

"I know." He kissed her. "I'll not forget this."

It would be good to get away for a day; it would be some activity. This waiting for Ross was pulling unbearably at her nerves.

"By the way," she said, "does Sam know yet?"

"Not yet. Could you tell him? I think, I reckon you'd do un better'n me."

III

Torrential December rain flooded the road near Marlborough, and Ross and Caroline's coach was held up for a day. Sunday the eighth they spent in Plymouth and knew that tomorrow they'd be home. They had dined together each day and supped together pleasantly each evening and had talked of many subjects from the insanity of the Czar to the tax on horses; but they had kept off personal issues. Ross found Caroline an agreeable companion, witty when she talked but economical of speech. She didn't have Demelza's small conversation.

They were sleeping at the Fountain Inn, and dining in one of the comfortable boxes with the red plush seats and walnut tables; and eventually it was Ross who for the first time drew aside the polite veil that had existed between them. He reminded Caroline of the meeting he had contrived between Dwight and herself at this inn. It was scarcely more than six years ago, in fact.

"It seems half a lifetime," said Caroline. "And must seem more still to Dwight, covering as it does not merely his captivity in France but four years of marriage to me!"

"I have often wondered," Ross said, "at my arrogance in bringing you together almost by force, at my supposing I knew better than you and he whether you should become husband and wife."

"The trouble is, Ross," she said, "that

you're an arrogant man. Sometimes it is a great virtue and sometimes not.''

''Well, which was it on that occasion?''

She smiled. She had changed for supper into a gown of cool green velvet, her favourite colour, because it contrasted with her auburn hair and brought out the green in her eyes, which could often with other colours look plain hazel or grey.

''A virtue,'' she said. ''Dwight is the only man I've ever wanted to marry . . . Though perhaps not the only man I've ever wanted to bed.''

Ross cut up a piece of the mutton on his plate and added some caper sauce.

''I don't think that makes you unusual,'' he said.

''No . . . we all look elsewhere from time to time. But then we glance away.''

''Usually . . .''

She ate a little, picked at her meat.

She said abruptly: ''Dwight and I, you and Demelza; do you realise how moral we are by the standards of today?''

''No doubt.''

''No doubt at all. So many of my friends in London . . . But forget London.

This county we live in. Add up the number of affairs that are going on, some secret, some blatant, among our friends, or their friends. And the same, though perhaps to a different pattern, among the poor."

Ross took a sip of wine. "It has always been so."

"Yes. But also there has been always a small core of real marriages existing amongst the rest — marriages in which love and fidelity and truth have maintained their importance. Yours is one and mine is one. Isn't that so?"

"Yes."

Caroline took a long draught of wine, half a glass as against Ross's sip. She leaned back against the red plush. "For instance, Ross, I could lie happily with you tonight."

His eyes went quickly up to hers. "Could you?"

"Yes. In fact I've always wanted to — as perhaps you know."

"Do I?"

"I think so. I believe you could take me as few other men could take me —

matching my arrogance with your own.''

There was silence between them.

"But . . ." she said.

"But?"

"But it could not be. Even if you were willing. I have the instinct of a wanton but the emotions of a wife. I have too much love for Dwight. And too much love for Demelza. And perhaps even too much love for you.''

He raised his eyes and smiled at her. "That's the nicest compliment of all.''

The colour in her face came and went. "I am not here to pay you compliments, Ross, but only — I'm only trying to say some things that I think you should hear. If we got rid of Ellen — as we easily could — and spent *all* night making love, and if then the first time I went to Nampara I told Demelza about it, do you think she would be hurt?''

"Yes."

"So do I. But I am a good friend of hers now. We are deeply attached to each other. Perhaps in time she would forgive me.''

"What are you trying to say?''

"I'm trying to say that if I told her what had happened between us she would be hurt. But no more so, I believe, than you hurt her in London."

Ross put down his knife. "I don't understand that at all."

"You killed a man because of her. Oh, I know it was his challenge. And I know the quarrel was about some seat in the House. And I know you disliked each other from the start. But it was really because of her that you killed him, wasn't it?"

"Partly, yes. But I don't see — "

"Ross, when you fought Monk Adderley, it was not really him you were killing, was it."

"Wasn't it?"

"No . . . it was Hugh Armitage."

He took a gulp of wine this time. "Damn you, Caroline, it was a plain straightforward duel — "

"It was nothing of the sort, and you know it! You killed him because you couldn't kill Hugh Armitage, who died anyway. But Hugh was a gentle, virile, sensitive man — the only sort Demelza

831

would *ever* have, could *ever* have felt deeply drawn to. You must have known from the beginning that she wouldn't have spared so much as a *thought* for a wild worthless rake like Monk Adderley."

"Sometimes one doesn't think these things out."

"Of *course* one doesn't think them out — that's the trouble! Yours was a totally emotional act. But you were fighting the wrong man just the same."

Ross pushed his plate away and put his fingers on the table.

"And don't get up and leave me," she said "for I should consider that a piece of very ungentlemanly behaviour."

"I have no intention of getting up and leaving you. But I can listen better to your lecture if I am not eating."

"The lecture is over; so you may enjoy the rest of your supper in silence."

"After that I am not sure that I want to enjoy my supper either in silence or in seasonable conversation."

"Perhaps I should not have spoken."

"If you believed it, then you should. I am trying to think hard of what you've just said, to be — rational about it instead of emotional. D'you know you're the second person in two weeks to accuse me of making emotional decisions. You'll never guess who the first was. But so be it. Let me think . . ."

She toyed again with her meat for a few moments, broke a piece of bread with her long fingers but made no move to eat it.

He said: "There may be some truth in it. How am I to be sure? Certainly I've felt a lot, and thought a lot, about Demelza and Hugh these last two years. When I first found out about Demelza it was as if I had lost some belief — some faith in human character. It was not so much her I blamed as — as something in humanity. You must not laugh at me for sounding silly and pompous."

"I'm not doing so. But if — "

"It was like finding an absolute flawed. If something has driven me of late, there may be jealousy in it, but it is not *just* jealousy. At times I have discovered a new lowness of spirit, a new need to revolt, to kick against the constraints that a civilised life tries to impose." He stopped and regarded her. "Because what is civilised life but an imposition of unreal standards upon flawed and defective human beings by other human beings no less flawed and defective? It has seemed to me that there is a rottenness to it that I have constantly wanted to kick against and to overset." He stopped again, breathing slowly, trying to marshal the complexities of his own feelings.

"And this has all come — this has derived from your estrangement from Demelza?"

"Oh, not in its entirety. But one and the other. One and the other. You called me an arrogant man just now, Caroline. Perhaps one aspect of arrogance lies in not being willing to accept what life sometimes expects one to accept. The very *feeling* of jealousy is an offence to one's spirit, it is a degrading sensation and should be stamped on." He tapped the table. "But so far as Demelza and Monk Adderley were concerned, I think you do me some injustice. Demelza *did* give him encouragement, of a sort. She was always exchanging asides with him, making another appointment — or at least permitting him to. And she allowed him to paw her — "

"Oh, nonsense!" Caroline said. "It is Demelza's way to be friendly — to flirt a little out of sheer high spirits. Whenever she goes out, as you well know, some man or another is always attracted by her peculiar vitality and charm. When she is enjoying herself she can't resist giving off this — this challenging sparkle. And men come to it. And she enjoys that. But in all *innocence,* Ross, for God's sake! As you must know. Are you going to challenge Sir Hugh Bodrugan to a duel? He had made more attempts on Demelza's chastity than any other two men I know. What will you fight him with — walking sticks?"

Ross half laughed. "You must know that jealousy flares only when there is risk."

"And do you seriously think that Monk Adderley constituted a risk?"

"I . . . thought so. It was not as simple a choice as that. And in any event he challenged me, not I him."

Caroline shifted her position, and

stretched. "Oh, that coach has tired me! . . . One more day and we shall be home."

The waiter came and took away their plates but left the knives and forks for use again.

Ross said quietly: "Yes, I could sleep with you."

She smiled at him.

He said: "And for the same reasons will not."

"Thank you, Captain."

He said: "You've *always* been my firm friend — from *so* long ago. Almost before we knew each other well at all."

"I believe I fancied you from the beginning."

"I believe it was something more important than that, even then,"

She shrugged but did not speak as the waiter came back. When he had gone again she said: "Perhaps I have been hard on you tonight, Ross. . . . What a thing to say! Hard on *you! Strange* for me to be in this position! I've never before dared! Well, I understand — a little — how you must have felt about Hugh and Demelza. It has been — irking, festering in your soul for two years. And the rest too, if you will. I don't deny that a single disillusion, if deeply felt, can lead to a general disillusion. Well . . . But now the blood is let. Even if it be the wrong blood. Let us not discuss any more the merits or demerits of your quarrel with Monk Adderley. It is over and *nothing* can revive it. Well, so is your quarrel with Hugh Armitage. So should be your quarrel with humanity. And so should be your quarrel with Demelza. She has been desperately affronted by what happened in London. The rights and wrongs of it do not matter so much as that you killed a man because of her, *and* that you risked everything, your life, her life — in a way — for a senseless quarrel which to a well-bred person may seem the ultimate and honourable way of settling a difference but to a miner's daughter, with her sense of values so firmly and sanely earthy, looks like the petulance of a wicked man."

"God," said Ross. "Well, I will keep that in my heart and let that fester a while."

"You spoke to me straight six years ago," said Caroline. "I speak to you straight now."

"Out of love?" he asked.

She nodded. "Out of love."

CHAPTER XII

Early on the Monday morning Demelza and Drake left for Bodmin. Morwenna stayed at Pally's Shop. Mrs. Trewinnard had been spending each night in the cottage; during the day the Trewinnard twins were there to answer the bell. Morwenna had shown no desire to go out, being content to sit and sew or to help with the cooking or the housework. She and Drake had talked little, being content to exchange the occasional commonplace, each a little shy of the other. She was like a wounded wild animal he was trying to tame: he made no sudden move or attempt to touch her lest she take fright. At first he had thought her unwell, in spite of her denials, but she was not. Her spirit, he decided, was clouded and needed above all time to recuperate and rest.

They had not even been beyond the fences that marked the five acres that he owned. He showed her these with pride, and she asked him about his work, and when he was working watched with seeming interest. Sometimes she was downstairs when people brought things to the smithy, but she did not come out. They had not been to church yesterday, but at Demelza's suggestion the banns had been called for the first time. It did not matter that the news was out, and it was safer not to miss a week in case there should be some holdup at Bodmin.

On Saturday Sam had come to see them, and had been much taken with Morwenna's quietness and modesty, also by his brother's obvious elation. Drake knew he could not object to the wedding but had feared the qualifications in his voice and manner. They were not there. Indeed Sam at once perceived in this silent, quietly elegant girl potentially suitable material for conversion to his own flock. Admittedly, her all too close connections with the Church proper put her provisionally out of reach of the sort of Christian Message Sam brought; but she had suffered as a result of her first marriage, and might now very well not only prove to be a brand ripe to be snatched from the burning but a means of returning Drake to full membership of the Connexion.

Anyway that was in the future. For the present Sam looked on his brother's face and saw that it was good, and praised the Lord for something that was both a carnal and a spiritual joy. It was selfish and unworthy, he knew, to feel a little twist inside him as he tramped away to think how good it would have been if he could have had Emma too.

Monday was fine but heavily gusty. John Gimlett, who fancied himself a weather prophet, said there would be rain later, once the sun got round to the butt of the wind. What he should have noted was the way, far out in the distance, the sea tramped, glittering in the sun. Sea birds were coming inland.

Drake and Demelza left at eight, at about the time Ross and Caroline were passing through Liskeard. At eleven

Elizabeth called to see Morwenna.

She was upstairs working on the curtains that Drake had inelegantly hemmed when one of the indistinguishable Trewinnards put his beak round the door and piped: "If ee plaise, ma'am, thur be a laady to see ee."

Elizabeth came up the steps. Morwenna flushed, rose defensively, looked around as if seeking a way of escape, and, finding none, accepted the kiss. Elizabeth was her dearest cousin, who had connived at her marriage with Ossie. Although the chief pressure had come from George, Elizabeth had connived. However, over the last year or more Elizabeth had shown real sympathy. And after John Conan was born she had been the one to insist that Morwenna was not being treated properly by Dr. Behenna and that Dr. Enys be called in. She had also helped in whatever way she could after Ossie's death.

In the hostile life of the vicarage Morwenna would have greeted her as a friend. In this warm quiet retreat where, cocoon-like, Drake was hiding her, Elizabeth represented the enemy.

Elizabeth said: "But the banns were called yesterday! How could I not know? Is Drake not here?"

"No, he's out. Will you sit down?"

They seated themselves and looked at each other, Morwenna's eye not really seeing anything. After a few moments she remembered herself and said:

"Can I get you something — tea or hot milk? I'm afraid there's nothing stronger."

"No, thank you. Though I shall be glad to rest a few minutes. The wind is so blustery."

Morwenna looked at her cousin's figure. "You did not, surely, walk, now you are — "

"Of course. It does me good." Elizabeth unbuttoned her dark fawn cloak and allowed the hood to fall back. She tried to arrange her hair. "It is not very far to Trenwith, you know. Scarcely two miles. Perhaps you did not come this way when you lived there."

"Sometimes. Though I scarce remember this part. Most often it was the other way. Geoffrey Charles so often wanted . . ."

"I know, my dear, I know. That is all over and done with. It was a very sad period in our relationship. We did not know. We did not understand."

Morwenna thought how much older Elizabeth was suddenly looking. But perhaps it was the pregnancy tiring her, bearing her down.

"And now," Elizabeth said, "you are to marry Drake after all. And you are to live here?" She looked around. "Are the Poldarks pleased?"

Morwenna flushed: "I hope so."

"Have they not said so?"

"Captain Poldark is still away. I hope they will never have any reason to feel ashamed of me."

"That I would have thought very unlikely. And Lady Whitworth?"

"She was not pleased."

Elizabeth smoothed her frock to conceal the bulge that was there. "It must have been so very trying, living with her. One of the most formidable of old women . . . But you just told her you were leaving and left?"

"Yes."

"And — John Conan?"

Morwenna winced. "Yes also."

"You did not mind leaving your own *son?*"

"Yes . . . and no. Please do not ask me any more!"

"I'm sorry. I didn't wish to distress you."

"No . . ." Morwenna folded the curtain and put it down. "You see, I never felt he was really my child, Elizabeth. He was *Ossie's* child. Ossie's son. And I am convinced he will grow up exactly like his father!"

Outside someone was ringing the bell for attention. The wind leaned against the cottage and made it creak.

Elizabeth said: "You could never accept Ossie, could you. I'm — when I got to know him better I felt I could understand that. But I never liked to ask more personally at the time. If you ever want to talk about it . . ."

"No."

Elizabeth said: "But it must have been a great sacrifice to leave your only child. . . . You did not think to bring him?"

Morwenna stood up. "Elizabeth, in whatever way I cared for him as a baby — and of course I cared then — I do not want him now! He is a *Whitworth!*"

Elizabeth stared out of the small window at the tossing trees. For no very good reason except the bitterness in Morwenna's voice, a reflection of something else seemed to show in the defective pane. It was a bottle of cloudy brown medicine that had come in the coach all the way from London, jogging in her luggage but not breaking. It had become a symbol, a bitter symbol of the disintegration of her own marriage. *He is a Whitworth! He is a Poldark!*

"You will not, of course, stay here all the time until you marry?"

"There is a woman comes in every night. I am — chaperoned."

"No, no, Morwenna, you must stay at Trenwith! It is only proper. You could have your old room."

"Oh, no, thank you!"

Elizabeth frowned, a little offended. "You were married from Trenwith last time. Why not this?"

"And have Mr. Warleggan give me away?"

Elizabeth looked up at this sarcasm from so gentle a creature.

"Mr. Warleggan is in Truro and like to remain there. He may come for Christmas. Shall you be able to be married before Christmas?" Elizabeth counted. "Yes, just. What day is Christmas Day — Wednesday? You could be married perhaps Christmas Eve."

"Perhaps." Morwenna could not bring herself to explain where Demelza and Drake had gone today. Elizabeth would say, what is the hurry; you are both still young; after waiting all this time, where is the haste? She might even persuade Morwenna. That was the worst danger — that her opinion would prevail.

Elizabeth said: "I had hoped to see Drake. Will he be long?"

"Quite a time, I fear."

"I wanted to meet him again so that there should be no hard feelings between us."

"I don't think there is," said Morwenna. "I think he admires you.

847

For what you did for him once."

Elizabeth coloured. "I had forgot that . . . It was little enough." She rose. "So I must see him some other time, for I think we're in for a storm and I should not want to be caught in it. Morwenna . . ."

"Yes?"

"Would you not come to Trenwith sometime? My mother and father are both still there and are both much devoted to you. They're very frail now, but I'm sure they would want to see you before your marriage — just to wish you well."

"Of course." The two women kissed, with a slightly greater warmth, at least on Morwenna's side, than when they had met.

They went down into the kitchen and Morwenna opened the door. It was torn from her grasp and flung back on its hinges. The wind gulped its way into the kitchen, knocking over a bottle and a pair of scales.

"My dear!" said Elizabeth. "It has doubled in force since I came. Fortunate that it will not be entirely in my face as I go home."

"Wait a while. This is perhaps a brief violence and will subside."

"I've lived too long on this coast to believe that! It may well blow for twelve hours. No, I can manage."

"You might fall. In your condition . . ."

"Would it matter?"

Morwenna drew a little back to look at her cousin. "I don't know what you mean."

Elizabeth tried to cover the slip. "I mean I think it would do me no harm."

"But did you not fall last time?" Morwenna's naturally warm nature forced its way through the veil of preoccupation that was obscuring her mind. "Wait. I'll come partway with you."

"No, no. Look, it is just the door where it is so bad. Once out in the yard . . ."

"Two will be stronger than one. I'll get my cloak."

As they were struggling out of the yard Morwenna called to one of the Trewinnard boys. "I am just taking Mrs. Warleggan back to Trenwith."

"Ais'm."

It was a long struggle, with a raving southwest gale just gathering strength and buffeting them this way and that. Quite clearly Morwenna could not turn back until Elizabeth was safely home, right up to the door of Trenwith. There Elizabeth said, since Morwenna had come so far, surely she would just slip in for a moment to greet her father and mother. Morwenna said, well, just at present she would really rather not. Elizabeth said, I think they would be hurt to know you had come right to the door and not seen them. With a shiver of remembrance, Morwenna stepped into the big, picture-hung hall. Then, with the wind ranting outside and rattling the great leaded window as if it would pull it down, she accepted their invitation to stay to dinner.

II

The gale of December the ninth, 1799, was little worse than a half dozen others that might occur most years; but it was distinguished by the great seas it brought in. The worst of the storms had been far out in the Atlantic, and the coast suffered the effects. Nine ships of varying size were wrecked, mainly along the south coast, and particularly in the area of the Manacles, but a few came to grief along the north coast. Hendrawna Beach drew a blank.

Various people were converging on the area of Sawle-with-Grambler as the day progressed. Ross and Caroline had caught the new express coach that left Torpoint at seven-thirty and was due in Truro soon after midday. The gale delayed the coach, and two o'clock had gone when, after a brief and early dinner at the Royal, they mounted their hired horses for the last stage.

Demelza and Drake had reached Bodmin in fair time, but the Reverend John Pomeroy, rector of Lesnewth, vicar of Bodmin, and the Archdeacon's representative, was out and did not return until noon. Although he then raised no obstacles to the issue of a licence, it was time enough when the formalities were completed; and even then Drake had another call to make before they turned for home.

The other notable riding towards the north coast was Mr. George Warleggan.

The first to reach his destination, if one excepts Caroline and her maid, whom he left at the gates of Killewarren, was Ross. Like his wife's a few weeks earlier, his arrival was unannounced and unexpected. The first person who saw him was a thin, long-legged eight-year-old boy staggering across the garden carrying a ball of twine. His scream was lost in the scream of the wind, but soon he was in his father's arms and soon there was all the confusion that had attended Demelza's return. In the midst of it Ross asked where his wife was and was told that Mama had gone off with Uncle Drake early this morning and had said she would not be back to dinner.

"Daddy!" Jeremy shouted, above the chatter of his sister and the welcome of the servants. "Daddy, come and look at the *sea!*"

So they all went to look, at least as far as the stile leading down to the beach; further it was unsafe to go. Where the beach would have been at any time except the highest of tides, was a battlefield of giant waves. The sea was washing away the lower sandhills and the roots of marram grass. As they stood there a wave came rushing up over the rough stony ground and licked at the foot of the stile, leaving a trail of froth to overflow and smear their boots. Surf in the ordinary sense progresses from deep water to shallow, losing height as it comes. Today waves were hitting the rocks below Wheal Leisure with such weight that they generated a new surf running at right angles to the flow of the sea, with geysers of water spouting high from the collisions. A new and irrational surf broke against the gentler rocks below the Long Field. Mountains of spume collected wherever the sea drew breath, and then blew like bursting shells across the land. The sea was so high there was no horizon and the clouds so low that they sagged into the sea.

As he steered his chattering family back into the house Ross tried to discover what their mother was about being away all day in this fashion, but nobody seemed to know. Then Jane Gimlett drew him aside and whispered in his ear. Ross nodded and looked out at the lowering sky. Once again something important had happened in his absence. She should have been home before this, and in less than an hour it would be dark.

Gimlett had taken his horse to the stables, and, after a glass of ale, he patted his children's eager faces and said he was going out and would be back in half an hour and, alas, it was too windy for them to come with him. So he went up to the mine and saw Zacky Martin and some of his other friends, and as he moved to return to the house he saw Drake riding away up the valley. Avoiding a meeting at this stage, he stood behind one of the sheds until he was past and then walked down.

Demelza, having heard of his arrival, had come quick again to the door and was peering into the dark afternoon looking for him. They saw each other, and she came as far as the edge of the garden to meet him; almost breaking into a run but then checking herself.

She stopped, uncertain.

He said: "Well, Demelza . . ."

"Are you — " she said. "Did anything happen?"

"When?"

"After I left, of course."

"No, the incident is dead."

She said: "Oh . . ."

"An unfortunate choice of words, perhaps."

"No," she said. "The incident is — dead."

"Though it will live a long time in my mind."

There was a pause.

He bent and kissed her. Her lips were cool and tentative.

"Have you been back long?"

"Less than an hour. I came with Caroline. The coach was late."

"What a day . . ."

They stared about them, glad of a subject they could share without emotion. Foam blew in soap suds about the garden and hung in tattered streaks from brambles and branches like the seeds of wild clematis.

Ross said: "This is why some of those pretty trees from Strawberry Hill would not grow here."

"Even those that are growing here look in a poor way."

"When I got home Jeremy was trying to tie some of them up."

"Was he? He loves plants. This morning it was only normal gusty. I have been to Bodmin with Drake."

"Jane told me."

"I'll explain it all later. Have you eaten, Ross?"

"Briefly and early. But I can wait till supper."

At the moment each was content with a neutrality founded on the exchange of commonplaces, the incidence and occurrence of mundane things. If there was to be war or peace between them, love or lost love, agreement or disagreement, affinity or misunderstanding, it must yet wait a while to emerge. The sharp edges could be cushioned for a time by the routine of home.

They turned and went into the

house together.

With the licence in his belt Drake was meanwhile making his way towards Sawle. Demelza had lent him Judith until tomorrow, so he was in time at Parson Odgers's cottage to catch him and his eldest son hammering at a piece of guttering that had come down in the gale. Drake was feeling so benevolent to the world in general that he said he would come up so soon as ever the gale had abated and replace all that piece over the front door with a piece of new. What they were putting back, he said, had gone poor and would hardly see the winter out.

He did not intend this as an ingratiating gesture, but Parson Odgers did seem to feel that there might be more in the young man than he had previously noted; he peered at the licence through a pair of broken spectacles, said all was in order and when did they now wish to be wed; next Monday? Drake said, could it be earlier than that? Parson Odgers said, well, there was nothing to stipulate that it should *not* be earlier; when did the young man suggest? The young man suggested tomorrow. Odgers winced as if he had been trodden on and said, impossible, he was busy tomorrow; he had appointments, all sorts of things to see to; couldn't manage that. Perhaps, if he rearranged his schedules he might be able to fit it in on Wednesday morning. Drake, having observed the unintended effect of his offer to replace some of the guttering, said, well, if by some chance Mr. Odgers could fit them in any time tomorrow, didn't matter whether twas early or late, he would, could, easily repair the whole of the guttering of the cottage before the end of the winter. He'd got some very suitable iron that could soon be knocked into shape and given a coat of paint before it was put up. Heavy stuff that would last for years. Mr. Odgers coughed into his woollen scarf and said: ''Two-thirty, then.

''Mind you're not late,'' he added, as Drake turned happily away. ''I can't celebrate after three. It's against the law.''

''Thank you, Mr. Odgers. Rest sure we'll not be late. Reckon we shall be in church soon after two.''

"Two-*thirty*, I said! And that, of course, is dependent on the gale. In this climate my poor church has so much to stand."

As he mounted Judith, Drake offered up a silent prayer that Sawle's leaning spire should resist at least one more storm. The gale was becoming a little less violent with the onset of dusk. That was not saying much; Judith staggered under the constant buffeting, and even here, two hundred feet above the sea, puffs of foam drifted like ghosts, dodging and dipping in the wind.

It had been a long day for Drake following other long days, but there was no fatigue in any of them. He had slept barely three hours any night since Morwenna came but he had felt no sleepiness during the day, nor did now, nor would when he put his head down. If there had been need he would cheerfully have ridden the fifty miles to Bodmin and back all over again. Life was in him like a burning, glowing spark; every moment, every thought added breath to it, fanning it alive. Ross had said to him once:

"Nothing should be able to destroy your life like that." But it had. Perhaps equally nothing — no one person — should have been able to *make* his life like this — to make it over again, in Sam's terms. But it was so. And if the depths were too deep, surely no heights could be too high. There might be a moral law against misery: there was none against happiness.

Nor did he feel any serious doubts about Morwenna's love for him. At the moment he had no thoughts beyond securing her in wedded companionship: let the rest come if or when it would. He was prepared to be as patient as he promised — to wait for months or years. What did it matter if it *was* half a marriage? There was a proverb that among the blind the one-eyed man was king. Until a few days ago he had been blind.

At the top of the last long hill he dismounted, for Judith was very tired. He led her down the narrow track, noticing with some surprise that there seemed to be no light in Pally's Shop. Indoors it must surely be dark by now, and Morwenna, if she were sewing, should not be straining her eyes. A worm of alarm moved in him. But then, of course, she might be at the gate waiting for him. She should be the one who might be worried.

But she was not at the gate. The place looked deserted. The Trewinnard boys normally worked from dawn until dusk, but on a day like this he would have sent them home by three. Had they gone? And had Morwenna gone? He jumped off the pony, looped the reins over the post, and ran into the house.

"Morwenna! Morwenna!" Through the kitchen up to the parlour, and then partway up the ladder to the bedrooms. Nobody. The fire was out. Nothing. He was back to what he had been a week ago. He climbed the rest of the way and looked in at the bedroom where she had been sleeping. There was her bag, her nightdress, her slippers, her brush and comb. So at least she could not have —

"If ee plaise, sur." One of the Trewinnards, he didn't know which. "Mistress Whitworth, sur, she'm gone out."

"*Gone* out? Where?" Relief of a sort.

"Gone Trenwith."

"Trenwith?" No relief now.

"Mistress Warleggan came for she this morning. Mistress Whitworth say she will walk her 'ome, as Mistress Warleggan be carren a baby, and in this gale o'wind."

"When was this, Jack?"

"Jim, sur. Jack be gone. We tossed a coin to see who'd stay till one of ee was 'ome. Oh . . . dunno. Aven no wa-atch. Twould be afore noon, reckon."

"Did she say — *anything* more — how long she'd be?"

"Nay, sur, naught more'n I d'say. She just say she be gwan walk Mistress Warleggan 'ome. I reckoned she'd be no more 'n a 'our."

"Thank ee, Jim. Go home now."

"Ais, sur."

Barely stopping to slam the door behind him, Drake ran for the tired pony, clambered on its back, dug his heels in, and turned madly up the hill towards Trenwith.

CHAPTER XIII

As soon as she sat down to dinner Morwenna regretted the decision to stay. It had been very hard to refuse and would have seemed like a rebuff to the two old people welcoming her. It would, too, have been a rebuff to Elizabeth, who, however misguided earlier, had made what amends she could. Especially she had befriended Drake on an issue of great importance to his survival as a smith. It was good also to see that darkly attractive little boy, Valentine Warleggan, again. On their visits in Truro Morwenna had seen a good deal of him and become fond of him. He sat beside her at the meal, and plied her with more food and drink than she could eat.

That was all right; but this house was darkly reminiscent of trouble and bitter scenes and heartbreak. Merely being in it put back the clock to the time when she was Geoffrey Charles's governess and an impressionable girl in her teens, likely to be overborne by her elders. It served to undermine her conviction now. Now that she was here, nothing seemed as definite, nothing as decided. She told herself that this was a weakness within herself, created by the nervous strains of these last years; irresolution was not deep in her temperament. Yet it was deep in her consciousness.

Nor, now that she had stayed, did she feel she had had the need to for fear of offending the old Chynoweths. Though they knew her to be a widow and had had a child of her own, they were not really interested in her or concerned about her affairs. The four years since she left Trenwith as a modest bride might have contained a whole lifetime for Morwenna; to them it was a few months in a repetitive existence whose monotony was only broken by the variety of the ailments they suffered. And their welcome to her was not really based on any personal warmth but on the recognition of a familiar human being who in the past had always been willing to sit and listen sympathetically to their complaints.

They had finished their main course and the heavy dishes were just being borne away when George arrived.

First it was a noise at the door and distant voices and the sound of feet. Then voices nearer and the clop of hooves on the gravel near the window. Elizabeth rose, her face flushing, put her hand on the back of her chair. George came in.

He was in tall boots and a snuff-coloured riding suit, and he was handing his cloak and hat to a servant as he entered. His hair was blown about by the wind, and he put up a hand to smooth it. His face was unusually red from its buffeting.

"Well, well," he said. "The family at dinner. Am I late?"

"Not in the least," Elizabeth said. "It can all be brought back straightaway. Stevens, Morrison . . ."

"Yes 'm."

"And Morwenna," said George, looking

across as he greeted his mother-in-law. "I had not thought to find you here."

"Just a visit," said Elizabeth. "What a day! What brought you in such weather?"

"Impulse. And I felt I should look to my affairs — "

"Papa! Papa! Did you get near blown away? — "

"And Valentine," said George sarcastically. "What a happy family!"

"Papa! Did you see the sea? It is e-*nor*-mous! Tom and Bettina took me to look down into Trevaunance Cove!"

"It is almost six months since I was here," George said, "and sometimes the presence of the owner has a salutary effect on the servants." He sat opposite Morwenna and glanced around him. "Ah . . . well, no, I think the cod is not for me, Stevens. Nor the fried beef. Was the goose good?"

"I did not eat it," said Elizabeth. "Father . . ."

"Eh? what? Oh, yes, the goose was fair enough. We'll need bigger than that for Christmas, though. There's few enough of any size about. The bad spring seemed to start 'em off late."

"Papa! They say the roof came right off Hoskin's cottage! Just like stripping a wig off a bald man! That's what Bettina said. Just like stripping a wig off a bald man!"

"Are you settling down with Lady Whitworth?" George asked Morwenna, ignoring the little boy. "No doubt you will find the life somewhat constricting."

"Well, no," said Morwenna, and stopped.

"Papa! — "

"Valentine," Elizabeth said, "please do not talk so much at the table. Allow your father a little peace."

"Peace," said George, still not looking at Valentine, "is something we prize only when it is lost. Like faith, like trust, like confidence." He began his dinner.

Elizabeth motioned to the butler to bring in the next course for the rest of them. It consisted of cherry tarts, mince pies, apple fritters, and a plum pudding, with cream and custard and jelly. Dinner went on for a while to the sound of the buffeting wind. George's presence was big and alien and dominant in the room, like that of a king who had just come into a group of his subjects. Everyone strove to behave normally and no one quite did.

Morwenna looked at Elizabeth, caught her eye, and indicated that she would like to leave. Elizabeth made a little warning negative movement of the head.

"From what I could see," said George, "the gardens are in poor state. What have the men been doing?"

"It is difficult to keep a place tidy at this time of year. And in this wind. I see a branch of the fir by the gates is hanging."

"The whole tree should come down. Have the apprentices arrived?"

"Yesterday in the forenoon."

"They cost me fifteen pounds each. It was too much, I thought, coming from a poorhouse, but the overseers said they were apty young boys."

"They seem so. But one, George, one called Wilkins, I would not allow in the house as he hadn't had the smallpox. He will have to sleep in the village."

"Oh, George," said Mrs. Chynoweth,

digging into her immediate memory and struggling with her unruly tongue. "Did you th-know that our little Morwenna is to wed again?"

Morwenna stared at the old woman in horror: during the whole of her visit this had not even been mentioned before. She had been given no idea that Mrs. Chynoweth even knew.

"No," said George, and laid down his knife to take a sip of wine. "That might be a way out of your present difficulties. Who is to be the man?"

"Papa," Valentine said, "I have been doing some painting in that picture book you bought me in London. You have to have the book quite flat or the colours run. I'll show you when I get down. Mama, might I get down?"

"No, dear, not yet . . ."

"The United States," said Mr. Chynoweth, half waking from a doze. "That's what they call themselves. A democracy. Hah! But what does their president say about it, what does he say? Eh? I'll tell you. He says, 'Remember, there never was a democracy that did not commit suicide.' That's what he says. What's his name? I forget. Adamson or Adams or some such."

An accumulation of the gale leaned against the house and seemed about to push it over. A footman came in and took away plates.

Elizabeth said: "That silver coffeepot we bought in London: one of the hinges of the lid is defective, I believe. I think we should take it back."

"I paid twenty-six pounds for it," said George.

"Your old horse, Kinsman has been ill with the butts," Elizabeth said. "A bottle of Daffy's Elixir has brought him a little better, but I fear it is partly his age."

"Let him be put down," said George.

"Papa," said Valentine, "The day we arrived such fun! We had scarce got into the house when a hawk was chasing a sparrow and the sparrow flew into the big hall through the open door and hid under the sideboard with the hawk following right into the house. Such a commotion! All the servants beating about! And in the end away flew the sparrow with the hawk still after him!"

There was a silence while they all listened to the wind.

Elizabeth said: "Farmer Hancock called yesterday. He was concerned to renew the lease on the 30 acres that you rent him. He says at present he pays thirty-five pounds a year."

"Hancock should know better than to call on you with his troubles," said George. "Tankard will be here next week."

"I didn't know that. I didn't know, of course, that you were coming."

Silence again.

"Who is to be the man?" George asked Morwenna.

Morwenna looked at him with sightless eyes.

"Lucy Pipe came back with the th-news from th-church yesterday," said Mrs. Chynoweth. "Th-some name. A carpenter or smith or th-some such. Not a good match, I th-should say. I don't know what her mother will think."

"Is it Carne?" George said, still looking directly at Morwenna.

"Papa," Valentine said. "When dinner is over, will you come up and let me show you — "

"Stevens," George said, turning to the butler, "please take this child away."

There was a brief stormy interlude while Valentine, tears in his eyes but not falling, was led away.

After the commotion had settled George said: "Is it Carne?"

Morwenna continued to look back at him. "Yes," she said.

II

Near Trenwith gates a gust of wind almost had pony and rider over, so Drake jumped off and ran beside Judith up the gravel drive. It seemed a long way, but his anxiety swamped fears of meeting the gamekeepers. He reached the front door. He hitched Judith to a post and pounded on the door. It was no time now for courtesy or finesse.

A man at length opened it, and held it open a bare three inches as the wind thrust to be in.

872

"Yes?"

"Is Mor — is Mrs. . . . Is — I came for Mrs. Whitworth."

The light showed up Drake's clothes. "Go round to the back door."

This door was closing. Drake put his foot in it. "I've come to see Mrs. Whitworth. Miss Chynoweth that was. She did say as she were coming here about noontime." He hesitated. "Be Mrs. *Warleggan* here?"

"You get round to the back, my man, where you belong, or else . . ."

"Can I see Mrs. Warleggan, please."

A struggle developed in the doorway. A door beyond opened, and more light came out.

"What is it, Morrison?"

"A man, sur — "

The door went back and the wind screamed like mad children and rushed round the hall.

"Begging your pardon, Mr. Warleggan," said Drake, his face tight. "I've no wish nor want to intrude, but I've heard that Morwenna's come up here and I've come for her."

"Carne," said George. "You are trespassing on this property. The law of trespass is a severe one, and I am a magistrate. I give you three minutes to be off my land." He took out his watch. "Then I'll send my gamekeepers after you."

Elizabeth came out of the room behind him. Her face was stretched with controlled emotion.

"Oh, Drake is it?" she said. "You must have — "

"Ma'am, I'm seeking Morwenna. If — "

"She's gone. Not ten minutes since."

A child was shouting upstairs and a door banged violently.

"Gone? Where? Where, ma'am?"

"She left. I thought she was — "

"On her own?"

"Yes, she would not stay — "

Drake said: "I just come from my shop. I've not seen her on the way."

"You have two minutes," said George. "And if you doubt my wife's word I shall rescind that, you insolent puppy. As for that dim-sighted slut you intend to marry,

I'll see she never enters this house again. Nor will she have any connection with anyone here! D'you *understand!* If she comes on this land I'll have her whipped off for a beggar!"

"Drake," said Elizabeth. "If you came by the drive . . . She may have taken the shortcut."

"Only ten minutes since?" He hesitated. "Thank ee, ma'am. *Thank* ee, ma'am."

Trembling with anger and anxiety, Drake turned again and went out. Before he was through the door it shut behind him, knocking him down the steps. He grabbed Judith and mounted her again, riding now into the teeth of the gale.

Elizabeth must be telling the truth. But even if she'd left, had she gone home? She might have wandered off somewhere. Even towards the cliffs. If George had treated her as he had treated him she would be desperately distraught. And the dark, and the low clouds, and this vile wind . . .

Kicking at the ribs of the pony, he reached the gates and began the struggle home.

Now that the tide was ebbing there was less spume to contend with; but still bits of twigs and dust and other light refuse flew intermittently, getting in Judith's eyes and making her ever more nervous. Few people were about even though it was yet early evening. Few would stir in such weather. A cottage here and there in the sheltered declivities of the land showed a gleam of light. Past Trevaunance the wind slackened.

Judith reared and nearly unseated him; it was a badger scuttling like an evil spirit across their path. Suppose Morwenna had fallen and he had missed her in the dark. He was superstitious about calling her name aloud as he rode. It might drive her away. She might not recognise his voice and cower in a ditch till he was past. Still worse, distressed by whatever had been said at Trenwith, she might have returned to the nervous mood in which she had rejected him in April, and refuse to answer.

He had to *see* her first, to see something moving. He prayed silently, but altogether without words.

The moon was rising, so it was not properly dark. The wind boomed overhead as if in an echoing, hollow tunnel from which all life had long since fled. The few harried trees nodded their heads against the breaking clouds. The land crouched in ungainly lumps and shadows, unfamiliar in the half-dark.

Down the last hill, which was the sharpest of all, and he got from the pony again as they went down, slithering and slipping among the mud and the stones. Pally's Shop was still in darkness. A single light gleamed on the opposite hill. And then he saw her.

There was no doubt at all in his mind because she looked exactly as she had done when she first came last Thursday. Tall, mannish in her long cloak, with a shuffling walk. She was at the gate of the smithy.

He dropped the reins and ran on and called her name, but it was too gentle and the wind snatched at it and bore it away.

"Morwenna!" he shouted.

She heard him this time and turned,

but with the cloak over her hair it was too dark to see her face.

"Drake."

He said: "I been *searching* for you and *searching* for you everywhere."

"Drake," she said, and hesitated, and then went into his arms.

He said: "I just been to Trenwith. They said you'd just left . . ."

"I was looking for you. I thought you weren't home." She was trembling and out of breath, exhausted.

"I must've missed you. Ye must've come through the wood."

"I came through the wood."

"Never fear, my love. Tis all past now. There's no need to worry no more."

He carefully did not kiss her or hold her against her will. But he noted that at this moment she was clinging to him.

III

George found Elizabeth in her bedroom, whence she had gone after quieting Valentine and talking to him and admiring his painting. George moved around the bedroom for a few moments, picking up one or two things and looking at them and then setting them down.

He said casually: "It is good to be in this house again. Having been absent so long one forgets its virtues."

Elizabeth did not reply, but examined a tiny blemish on her face.

George said: "A disagreeable ride and a disagreeable welcome. I fear I lost my temper downstairs."

"There was nothing disagreeable until you made it so."

He turned his head slowly, viewing her with quiet hostility. "You feel perfectly content that your cousin should be marrying that insolent, down-at-heel Methodist?"

"Not happy, no," said Elizabeth. "But before this we attempted to guide her, and perhaps we guided her wrong. Now there is nothing to be done. She is a woman — no longer a girl — and a widow, without ties, except those that her mother-in-law has accepted. We cannot control her, and it is stupid not to admit the fact."

"Stupid," he said. "I see. And is it not

stupid of you to have invited her there?''

''I hardly expected you to arrive today.''

''And that excuses it?''

''I don't consider any excuse is necessary,'' she said quietly.

''Ah, so that is it.''

''Yes . . . that is it.''

George recognised the steely sound in Elizabeth's voice which meant that she was willing for once to do battle. He realised that at this moment her anger was greater than his own. His had reached its peak downstairs when he had turned Morwenna out of the house, and was evaporating now into a sardonic ill-humour.

''You think it right that she should answer me in the way she did — that girl, that woman?''

''Do you think it right to say what you did to her? Implying that Drake Carne might have had some complicity in Osborne's death!''

''I said nothing of the sort. If she chose to take it that way . . .''

''You know it was investigated and

proved he was far away at the time."

"Oh, proved . . . One can prove anything. After all, Carne, it seems, stands to gain by the event."

"Sometimes I cannot understand you, George. You seem . . . driven on by something."

"Oh, yes, driven on. Sometimes I am driven on."

She took up her brush and began to touch the sides of her hair with it, arranging and adjusting the fine strands.

He made an effort. "I hope you've been well." But the words were cold.

"Quite well. Though scenes such as those downstairs make me feel no better."

"I'm sorry."

"*Are* you?"

He analysed his thoughts. "I am sorry that you upset yourself over what I said. I am not sorry to have turned that impudent creature out of the house, even if she is your cousin. Nor am I sorry to have sent her dishonest dandy boy packing."

"On the contrary," Elizabeth said. "I felt — degraded."

George flushed. He was struck in his

most vulnerable point. No Achilles could more obviously have possessed a heel through which his pride and confidence would escape.

"You have no *right* to say that!"

"You think not?"

"I *say* not."

He hacked the curtain aside and looked out. The moon was making the night light, and in Elizabeth's room, which overlooked the small courtyard, the wind was not strong enough to create a draught through the leaded panes. One more effort at some sort of conciliation.

He said with a dry laugh: "I have ridden here especially to see you, and we quarrel over two trivial people who concern us very little at all."

"There is one who does concern us both."

"Who is that?"

"Valentine."

He let the curtain fall. Elizabeth was sitting at her dressing table in a long flowing robe which hid the child she was bearing, and her slim shoulders and straight back seemed almost as girlish as when he had first seen them twenty years ago. The usual mixed emotions struggled within him when he looked at her. She was the only human being who could disturb him in this way.

"I have been — busy — scarce time to eat. I came here to *rest*. Valentine's prattle — annoys me."

"It is only the prattle of a normal boy. He was vastly upset tonight at being so dismissed."

George did not speak.

"Have you been in to see him since?" Elizabeth asked.

"No."

"Then you should."

George's neck stiffened all over again. Another reprimand. Ever since he came in this room everything she said had seen a reprimand. As if *she* were the master. As if *hers* were the money, the mines, the bank, the properties, the membership of the House, the business connections! It was *insufferable!* He could have struck her. He could have squeezed her neck between his fingers and silenced her in half a minute.

She turned and half smiled at him. "You should, George."

His feelings broke then, like a wave against the immutable rocks. And the immutability lay in his concern for this woman and what she thought of him.

"Elizabeth," he said harshly. "You know at times I am in torment."

"Because of the thoughtless words of *another* child?" She was bringing the issue into the open.

"Possibly. Partly. Out of the mouths of babes and sucklings . . ."

"So you think Geoffrey Charles in idleness points the truth, while all I have sworn to you before is false?"

He lowered his head like a goaded bull. "One does not *always* see these things in such precise terms. Let us say that at times I have been in torment; and then — then I speak my mind without concern for the courtesies of polite conversation. Then, no doubt, you reflect on the hazards of having married a blacksmith's son."

"I did not say that!"

"You said as good as that!"

"No, I did *not*. And if you are in

torment, George, how do you think I feel when you come into this house and ride roughshod over everyone and are violent to my cousin and cruel to our son? *Our* son, George! *Our* son! No, I do not think I have married a blacksmith's son, I think I have married a man who still carries a terrible weight upon his shoulders, a terrible evil weight of jealousy and suspicion that *nothing* and *nobody* can remove! Not anything I say! Not anything I have sworn! Not anything I may *do!* You will carry this black load for evermore and ruin the rest of our married life with it! . . . If there *is* to be more to our married life? . . ."

George looked into the darkness of his own soul and knew that she spoke the truth. He collected his temper, struggled with it, strove to put it aside. "Yes, well; we have had all this out before."

"So I had thought!"

"It is not a pretty subject. Old Agatha laid a curse upon our marriage, I believe, and — "

"Agatha?" She turned swiftly. *"Aunt* Agatha? What has she to do with this?"

He brooded a moment. "I had not intended ever to tell you . . ."

"I think it is time you told me, whatever there is to tell!"

He still hesitated, plucking at his lip. "No matter now."

"Tell me!"

"Well, the night she died she — when I went up to tell her she was only ninety-eight and not a centenarian as she pretended — she turned on me — I believe it was out of spite, out of revenge . . ."

"*What* did she say?"

"She said that Valentine was not my child."

Elizabeth stared at him, her face bitter.

"So *that* was where it all came from. . ."

"Yes. Most of it. All of it, I suppose."

"And you believed *her?* You believed a half-demented old woman?"

"She said you had not been married long enough to me to bear the child to its full term."

"Valentine was *premature.* I fell on the stairs!"

"So you said . . ."

"So I *said!* You still think, then, in spite of *everything* I've told you, that I have been living a deliberate lie ever since Valentine was born? That I never *fell* down the stairs, that I made it all up, to pass off Valentine as your child when he was *not!* Did Aunt Agatha tell you all that too?"

"No. But that was clearly what she meant. And why should she say anything of the sort? — "

"Because she *hated* you, George, that is why! She hated you just as much as you hated her! And how *could* she hate anyone more than you, when you had just ruined her precious birthday celebrations! She would say anything, anything that came into her head to damage you before she died."

"I thought you were fond of her."

"Of course I was!"

"Then why should she say something that might spoil your life just as much as mine?"

"Because hurting you was more important to her than anything else at that moment. It *must* have been! It was a *vile* trick of yours to ruin everything for her — "

"No trick! It was the truth!"

"Which no one need have known but for you! If you had come to see me first I would have besought you to say nothing about it. The celebration would have gone off, and everyone would have been happy, and in a few months Aunt Agatha would have passed peaceably away, content with her great triumph. But no! You had to go up and see her and tell her — you had to exact your cheap and petty revenge on her! So she tried to fight back, to hit you back with any weapon she had. And she could see that you were happy in your child; this was your great pride, that you had a *son,* a son to follow you and succeed to all your possessions. So she had to try and destroy *that.* I don't suppose it ever entered her head to consider me — or Valentine. Her one aim was to revenge herself on *you!* . . . And she did, didn't she? She succeeded!" Elizabeth laughed harshly. "She succeeded more than she could ever have imagined! Ever since then the venom has been working in your veins, and it will go on working till the day you die! What a revenge, George, what a revenge she scored on you, all because of your mean little triumph! Every day you've lived since then has been destroyed for you by Aunt Agatha!''

The sweat was standing out on his face. "God damn you, how dare you say anything like that to me! Mean and petty, you call me. Cheap and petty. I'll not suffer such insults!'' He turned as if to walk out of the room. "I sought to set things to rights about her age, that was all. Trust a Poldark to be cheating — ''

"She didn't know it!''

"I suspect she did.'' At the door he turned again, came back to the dressing table. "And what you have said to me tonight, Elizabeth — apart from such unforgivable insults — is totally untrue! It is not true that Agatha has poisoned my life ever since she died. Elizabeth, stop laughing!''

Elizabeth had her knuckles to her mouth, trying to control her laughter, the hysteria. She hiccuped, and coughed and laughed again, then retched.

"Are you ill?"

"I think," she said, "I'm going to faint."

He came quickly behind her as she swayed, caught her shoulders, then round the waist. As she slipped out of the chair he gathered her, picked her up with a grunt, looked down at her clouded eyes, carried her to the bed. She lay back, colour returning slowly, her fine fair hair, a little brazen from its recent tintings, coiled about her as it had fallen down, gleaming in the candlelight like a tarnished lake.

"What is it? What's the *matter?*" His anger was different now, deriving from alarm and not ill-temper. But it sounded little changed.

"It's nothing."

"It must be something! What can I get you? I'll ring for Ellen."

"No . . . The smelling salts. The drawer . . ."

He got them and waited. For a while neither spoke, and the interval allowed their passions to cool. Presently he moved away, stood with his back to the fire staring across at the bed.

She took another sniff and sighed. "My child moved — and there was pain."

"You'd best have a doctor," he said shortly. "Though God knows who to have in this benighted district! Choake is a cripple now, and that fellow Enys is too superior by half . . ."

"I shall be all right."

"We'll go back to Truro as soon as Christmas is over. Or before. It's safer with Behenna close by."

"You upset me greatly," she said. "I was very well."

He thrust his hands into his pockets. "It seems that I am a bad influence."

"Indeed you are."

"So I should go again, eh?"

"I don't wish you to go, but I cannot stand another scene like this."

"You perhaps would rather prefer I behaved like your first husband, going with light women, drinking myself stupid, gambling my money away . . ."

"You know I would not."

"So there are disadvantages to the fact that I care, eh? That it matters to me what you do and what you have done?"

She did not reply, and he stood over her, the conflict in himself still unresolved but aware that he could air it no farther. His anxiety about her health made it necessary for him to make a peaceable end of the quarrel, but he did not know how.

"I'll go and see Valentine," he said grudgingly.

"Thank you."

"This damned house is *unlucky*," he said. "Always it seems our misfortunes have come here."

"What misfortunes have we had?"

"It is a wrong word. Everything I say today seems wrong . . ." He struggled with his resentment. "You know my — my fondness for you never wavers."

"It is hard to believe that!"

"Well, it's the truth!" Suddenly angry again, he shouted: "You *must* know it, Elizabeth! You're the only person I've ever cared about!"

"There's one way you can prove it."

"How?"

"Include Valentine in your love."

IV

After he had gone she lay and dozed for a while.

She had genuinely felt ill and been afraid she would faint. The child had been very restless, and the passion of the quarrel had exhausted her. But after about an hour she got up and went into the next room and took a bottle out of her valise.

She knew it was nearly time for tea but she had asked not to be disturbed, and anyway she was not thirsty. She carried the bottle back to the bed, with a spoon, and unscrewed the cork and sniffed the reddish-brown liquid inside. A rather fusty smell, as of stale mushrooms. Then she put a spot on her tongue. It was not particularly unpleasant.

After seeing Dr. Anselm she had been on the point of throwing the bottle away. Eventually she had decided to keep it, but was sure she would never take it. As the time for taking it drew nearer this resolution had hardened. As she ailed frequently in small ways she had a decent respect for her own health, and she had no wish to damage it. Dr. Anselm had not disguised the fact that there was some risk, though he had not specified what the risk precisely was. Risk to the child, for one thing. She had no wish to risk its life. She hoped for a daughter. It seemed sometimes that she was surrounded by men. A little girl would be a joy and a comfort.

But George's manner tonight had shown that, even if he tried, he could *not* relinquish his old suspicions. Would a seven-month child now lay them for ever? He could not fail to be impressed. He could not possibly know of any artificial means she had resorted to to induce it. It *must* destroy his suspicions — surely. Even if Valentine grew up dark and tall and bony. A *second* premature child. He *could* not continue to harbour the old jealous fevers.

So, if she took the risk and all was well, she gained a stability for her own married life, but still more she was likely to ensure a normal life for Valentine. If he lived as he had lived intermittently these last years, as George's suspicions waxed and waned, he would grow up a nervous wreck. But if this ghost were laid for ever he could look forward to inheriting all that the Warleggans had built up for him. Nothing was dearer to Elizabeth's heart than the friendship which had grown between her first and her second son. If her first son — for whom she still cared most — was poor, and her second son was rich, and they loved each other, there could well be some interchange of interests and property which would enable Geoffrey Charles to live at Trenwith as its squire in the manner to which he should be entitled. Valentine, of course, was still very young and this was all in the future; but she would look forward to that future with a different vision if Valentine's position as George's heir were assured.

And this was the way of assuring it? It seemed so. There seemed no other.

She unstoppered the bottle again and put a drop of liquid into the spoon. It was quite a small bottle and it carried no label. The instructions were on a separate piece of paper in her handbag, and she knew them by heart. "Eight tablespoons of the liquid before retiring, during the second week of December. If the medicine fails to act, do not repeat."

V

A good deal later that evening, when the children were in bed, Ross asked Jane where his mistress was.

"She was out back somewhere, sur. Looking to the pigs, I b'lieve. But I think she've gone out by the back way. She thought to see the sea."

Ross put on his cloak and went to look for her. Whereas two hours ago he had hardly been able to stand, now it was only the occasional gust that made him stagger. The clouds had broken up and a brilliant moon two days from full was riding the sky.

He saw her standing by the old wall under the shelter of an outcrop of rock. It was the first place he looked because it was a favourite spot of hers from which to see the stretch of Hendrawna Beach.

He came up behind her, trying to make a noise with his boots so that he should not startle her. But all the same she started up.

"You made me jump!"

"I thought you might be here."

"Yes, I just came for a few minutes. I often do when you're away."

"I would have thought you'd have had enough fresh air today."

"I really came to look. Look at it."

With the tide more than half out, the beach lay tattered and broken in the moonlight, and covered with froth like the remnants of milk which has boiled away in a saucepan.

Ross said: "Thank God I didn't come home by sea."

"Thank God you didn't."

They stood there quiet for a while.

She said: "Nothing happened in London? There was truly nothing?"

"Nothing."

"That's . . . good to know."

"Mrs. Parkins was upset when you left so sudden. She thought you did not like the room."

"I trust you told her different."

"I told her you did not like me."

". . . That would not be exactly true."

Conversation dropped.

He said: "Drake will wed tomorrow?"

"He wants to. If Mr. Odgers will do it."

"He'd better. For us."

"Has he any hopes this time? Mr. Odgers, I mean."

"I think I have contrived it. But of course it must come through the patron, so he must hear it officially first."

"I'm *that* glad! Especially for Mrs. Odgers and the children. It will mean him getting — what?"

"Two hundred a year. It will multiply his present stipend nearly four times."

"I'm glad," said Demelza again.

For a few moments the wind shouted them down.

"But much more I'm glad for Drake," she continued. "Much, much more, of course. You would not believe the difference in him. He's a new man. All the way home he was singing."

"D'you think it will work?"

"I do now. Now I've met her properly.

But I think in any case, Ross, if two people love one another the way they do, then it's best to marry whatever the future bring. Even if it all goes wrong in a few years, nothing will take away the years they've had. Being in love is the difference between being alive and not being alive."

"Yes," said Ross.

After a minute Demelza went on: "Drake is very — right thinking. Today, because we were going to Bodmin, we *had* to call and see Morwenna's mother on the way home and ask her for her permission. I tried to put him off, but no. That's why we were so late back."

"Did she give it?"

"I wish I knew the word to describe her. Is it 'pretentious'?"

"I would think it likely."

"Of course, at first it was all distress. 'My little Morwenna, throwing herself away . . .' But — for Drake's sake, Ross — I had to put on a pretence myself. I pointed out that Drake, in spite of him not being smart in dress or speaking, is no common smith. After I'd told her that his brother-in-law was a mine owner, a member of Parliament, and a partner in the new Cornish Bank in Truro she began to come round.''

Ross grunted. '' 'Pretence' is the word.''

''No, Ross, not all. But it all ended quite comfortable with her wiping away her tears and saying she was too prostrate to see us to the door, and Drake having the impudence to kiss her, and then he kissed both Morwenna's pretty sisters, and they saw us away. So perhaps in a fashion it was a good thing to do after all.''

''That other sister of hers,'' said Ross. ''I think I saw her in Truro today. *She's* a strange creature, if ever there was one. Dowdy clothes and a dowdy walk, but . . . somehow she draws the eye.''

''*Morwenna* can draw the eye,'' said Demelza. ''After all, she drew the eye of Ossie.''

''To everybody's ultimate ruin . . . But *she* does it in all modesty . . . Not the other sister . . . Not she. Are you cold?''

''No.''

''Demelza . . . I have brought you a small present.''

''Oh? Where? Where is it?''

"I'll give it to you tomorrow — or whenever the wedding is."

"Why do I have to wait?"

"I had intended it for Christmas. And then I had intended it for tonight. But then I remembered other times I had given you presents, and it seemed to me that this was too easy a way of buying myself back into your favour . . ."

"Do you think you need to?"

"Well . . . what was done in London was not well done."

She said: "Is it then perhaps your own favours that you should first seek?"

"Maybe. Maybe it's the same thing. But in either case it is too easy a way of setting things to rights. A present, a little money spent, and all is forgiven and forgotten. It won't do."

Moonlight briefly flooded the scene, and she looked up at the scudding sky.

She said: "I left you. I left you when I should not have done — while there was still danger."

"Perhaps it was the only thing you could do."

"At the time it seemed so. But

afterwards, when I got home I thought different. That too was not well done."

He said: "In the past sometimes, when we have had great differences, there have been occasions when we have talked them out. We have talked and argued back and forth, and in the end I believe come to some acceptable conclusion. But other times nothing has been said. Nothing much but a word or two of regret or understanding. And that too has served. I am not sure which is the proper way here. Sometimes I think talking, explaining, creates as much misunderstanding as it clears anyway. And yet we cannot resume, cannot go on as if nothing at all had happened."

"No, I don't think we can, Ross."

"What can I say to put it right? . . ."

"Perhaps not much. Perhaps that is the wisest. For what can I say in my turn?"

"Well, I don't know. In our lives before this we've each given the other cause for deep offence. This is not worse, and should in ways be less bad. Yet it cuts as

uts as deep."

They had reached the heart of the issue.

"This time," Ross said, "I'm the chief offender — maybe the only one. At least I plead no excuse."

"Oh, Ross, it is not — "

"Perhaps in the end one measures the quality of one's forgiveness by the quality of one's love. Sometimes my love has been lacking. Is yours now?"

"No," she said. "Nor ever will be. Tisn't love I lack, Ross, but *understanding.*"

"Understanding comes from the head; love from the heart. Which have you always believed to be the more important?"

"It isn't quite as easy as that."

"No, I know," he acknowledged slowly. "I *ought* to know."

The clouds were flying so fast it looked as if the moon were being thrown across the sky.

"Perhaps," she said, "we both care too much."

"It's a signal failing in two people who have been married fourteen years. But I think if we can admit that, it is a long way towards understanding."

"But caring," she said. "Doesn't that mean thinking of the other? Perhaps we have each done too little of that."

"In other words our love has been selfish — "

"Not *that* much. But sometimes — "

"So we must be more tolerant, each of the other . . . But how do we achieve tolerance without indifference? Isn't that a worse fate?"

After a minute she said: "Yes."

"Then what is your answer?"

"My answer?"

"Your solution."

"Perhaps we must just go on living — and learning, Ross."

"And loving," said Ross.

"That most of all."

CHAPTER XIV

Drake was round at Nampara by seven-thirty. Having told them the time of the wedding, he went off to see Sam. Demelza rode to see Caroline and asked her if she could borrow a dress for Morwenna, since Caroline was about the right height. She bore this away to Pally's Shop.

Problems here, for Morwenna, although she looked slim enough, was like her sister Rowella and fuller in the right places than she appeared, and Caroline's frock would not button. This had *all* happened before, but only Morwenna knew it. Four years ago sew and stitch, sew and stitch — then it was altering Elizabeth's wedding frock for her. So another marriage now, in even greater haste, *same* church, *same* cleric — only the man was different. A tight hold, keep a tight hold on overstrung nerves

But her quarrel with George Warleggan last night — the vile things, the evil insinuations against Drake — somehow it had broken some mental block — not the effect Mr. Warleggan intended. She had *defended* Drake — would with her life — and in so doing became clearer in heart and mind. Marriage — this marriage — was still a haven to be sought, where she could at last be at peace. But the conflict last night had emptied her heart of doubt.

Drake, with more subtlety than Demelza had given him credit for, was careful not to crowd her or fuss over her. He never asked her what had taken place at Trenwith. He went on with his work throughout the morning, and cooked them a light meal at twelve, and stared up at the cumulus castles over the sea and reckoned it would not rain until nightfall. So time passed, and the frock, a cream grosgrain with a few dashes of crimson ribbon, was somehow made to fasten, and Drake changed into his new jacket and soon after o'clock they all rode to the church. for them was Ross, and the two n and Mrs. Kemp to keep them in order, and Sam, and his mate Peter Hoskin, and Jud and Prudie — uninvited — and Caroline — unexpected — and three or four others who had heard about it and drifted in.

And at two twenty-five the Reverend and Mrs. Odgers came and the ceremony began, and in what seemed no time at all it was all over and the indissoluble bond was sealed. The married couple signed the register, and a few minutes later they were all standing in the crowded graveyard with its silent stones leaning this way and that, like broken teeth, the names on them erased by the wild weather and the occupants below long since mouldered and forgotten.

Demelza, wearing a new and rare painted cameo on her breast, repeated her invitation to Drake and Morwenna to come to Nampara for tea and cakes, but she knew they would refuse. Ross kissed Morwenna, and then Demelza did, and then Caroline and then Sam; Drake kissed Demelza and then his brother; Caroline also kissed Demelza and left Ross to the last. Much handshaking followed, before

Mr. and Mrs. Drake Carne moved off on their ponies for the short ride home.

"So it is done," Demelza said, holding to her hat, which threatened to take off. "It is done, Sam. It is what they have desired most in the world ever since they first set eyes on each other."

"God have set them to grow in beauty side by side," Sam said.

Demelza watched the two figures dwindling in size as they passed the gates of Trenwith. In ten minutes they would be home, alone, happy in their new-found isolation, sipping tea, talking — or perhaps not talking — wishing only to be together in companionship and trust. She turned to look up at her brother, who was shading his face with his hand, to follow the departing couple. The rest of the group were dispersing. Mr. and Mrs. Odgers, having taken obsequious leave of Ross, were on their way back to their cottage. Caroline was talking to Ross. Jeremy was picking some moss off a ͮbstone and trying to read the lettering. ͤ was hopping from one curb to ∴. Mrs. Kemp was talking to an acquaintance. The sky was streaked as if broombrushed; the cumulus clouds had faded into the sea, which roared as if it had swallowed them.

Clowance stepped on one curb near where Jud and Prudie were waddling off.

Jud said: "Careful, 'ow ee d'walk, my 'andsome. Put your feet wrong round yur, and a gurt big skeleton'll jump out an' bite yer toe!"

"Big ox!" said Prudie. "Take no 'eed of 'm, my dee-er. Step just wher ee d'wish — there's naught'll disturb ee."

They passed on, growling at each other, leaving Clowance thumb in mouth staring after them. When they had gone a distance she tiptoed carefully to the edge of the path and hurried back to her mother.

Demelza led her to Ross.

"Where's Dwight?" she said to Caroline. "I had hoped you would both come to tea."

Caroline wrinkled her brows. "I was telling Ross. Dwight was to have come with me but at midday he was summoned to Trenwith, and I have seen nothin

909

of him since."

"Probably one of the old people," Demelza said. "Dr. Choake is now so crippled with gout . . ."

"No," Caroline said. "It was Elizabeth."

There was a short silence.

"Did they say what it was?"

"No . . ."

Ross took out his watch. "Well, he's been gone three hours."

"It might be to do with her baby," said Demelza.

"I wondered that," said Caroline. "I hope not, because it would be premature . . . though I understand Valentine was premature."

There was another silence.

"Yes," said Ross.

II

George had found Elizabeth lying on the the floor of her bedroom about ten ~~ck that morning. She had fallen in a not hurt herself. He got her back and he was all for summoning a doctor at once, but she assured him she had come to no hurt. Only the fact that Choake was immobile and his dislike of Enys persuaded George to acquiesce.

But an hour and a half later she complained of pain in the back, and he at once sent a man for Dwight. Dwight came and examined her and told him she was in the first stages of childbirth. George sent a man galloping to Truro to fetch Dr. Behenna.

This time, however, Dr. Behenna was going to be far too late. Pains were constant, with scarcely any intervals of any length, and contractions were regular and severe. At three o'clock Elizabeth gave birth to a girl, weighing just five pounds, wrinkled and redfaced and tiny, with a mouth that opened to cry but seemed only capable of emitting a faint mew like a newborn kitten. It was hairless, almost nailless, but very much alive. Elizabeth's wish for a daughter had come true.

There was no proper nurse present, and Dwight had to make use of Ellen Prowse, Polly Odgers, and the slovenly Lucy Pipe

But all had gone well, there were no complications, and when he had tidied up a bit he went down to inform the proud father of his fortune.

George had endured horrible conflicting doubts and fears since ten this morning, and when Dwight told him he had a daughter and that mother and child were doing well, he went across and poured himself another strong brandy, the decanter clicking on the glass as he did so. For once in his life he had drunk too much.

"May I offer you something, Dr. — er — hm — Dr. Enys?"

"Thank you, no." Dwight changed his mind in the interests of neighbourliness. "Well, yes, a weak one."

They drank together.

"My wife has come through well?" George asked, steadying himself on a chair.

"Yes. In one sense a premature child is less strain on the mother, being that much ~~ller~~. But the spasms were unusually ~~~ nd~~ if this is the result of her fall ~~~~ have to take the greatest care over the next few weeks. I would advise a wet nurse."

"Yes, yes. And the child?"

"The greatest care for a while. There's no reason at all why she should not do perfectly well, but a premature child is always more at risk. I presume you will have your own doctor . . ."

"Dr. Behenna has been sent for."

"Then I am sure he will be able to prescribe the correct treatment and care."

"When can I go and see them?"

"I have given your wife a sleeping draught which will make her drowsy until this evening, and have left another one with Miss Odgers in case she needs it tonight. Look in now if you wish, but don't stay."

George hesitated. "The old people are just starting dinner. If you would care to join them . . ."

"Well, it's time I was home. I have been here near on four hours and my wife will be wondering what has become of me."

George said: "They are safe to be left now — without a doctor, I mean?"

"Oh, yes. I'll call again about nine this evening if you wish it. But I presume Dr. Behenna will be here before then."

"If he left promptly when summoned he should be here within the hour. Thank you for your prompt and efficient attention."

After Dr. Enys had been shown out, George hesitated whether to go in and tell the old people that they were grandparents again; but he reasoned that although they knew Elizabeth was in labour they would not expect anything so soon, and Lucy Pipe could be sent down to tell them later. His overmastering need was to see Elizabeth.

He put his glass down and went to the mirror, straightened his stock, patted his hair. He wiped the sweat from his face with a handkerchief. He would do. He had not felt like this before, so damnably anxious all day, now so damnably relieved. It was not right that one should be subject to this sort of emotional stress; de one feel vulnerable and ashamed. nt up and tapped on the door dgers opened it and he went in.

Elizabeth was very pale, but in some respects looked less exhausted than she had done after the long labour of Valentine's birth. As always her frail beauty was enhanced by recumbency. It seemed natural to her deceptive delicacy to be at rest. Her hair lay gilt-picture-framed about the pillow, and when she saw George she took a handkerchief to wipe her dry lips. In a cot before the fire a tiny thing kicked and stirred.

"Well, George," she said.

George said: "Leave us, Polly."

"Yes, sir."

When she had gone he sat down heavily and stared at her; emotionally tight.

"So . . . all is well."

"Yes. All is well."

"Are you in pain?"

"Not now. Dr. Enys was very good."

"It has all happened the second time. Just as before. And so quickly."

"Yes. But last time it was eight months. This time it is seven."

"You *fall,*" he said accusingly, "always you fall."

"I *faint.* It is some peculiarity. Yoᵀ

remember I even did it this year when the child was first coming."

"Elizabeth, I . . ."

She watched him struggling with words but did not help.

"Elizabeth. Aunt Agatha's venom . . ."

Elizabeth waved a weary hand. "Let us forget it."

"Her venom. Her venom has . . . Since she died — as you said yesterday — it has affected half my life."

"And half mine without knowing the cause."

"I am a self-sufficient man. Self-contained. As you know. It is very difficult for me to — to unburden myself to another. In such cases suspicion flourishes. I have given way to suspicion and jealousy."

"From which I have had small opportunity to defend myself."

"Yes . . . I know. But you must appreciate that I have suffered too." He hunched his shoulders and stared ⸻ingly at her. "And what I said that ⸻o years ago — oh, it's true ⸻. Love and jealousy are part of the same face. Only a saint can enjoy one without enduring the other. And I had good reason for suspicion — ''

''Good reason?''

''Thought I had. Helped by that old woman's curse, so it seemed. Now at last I can see I was wrong. Clearly it has done damage — to our marriage. I trust it's not beyond repair.''

She was silent, luxuriating for a moment in the absence of pain, of travail, the laudanum working gently to blur the sharper edges of existence. George had drawn his chair closer and was holding her hand. It was very unusual in him. In fact she had never known it before. So is the hard man tamed.

She said quietly: ''It is for you to decide,'' knowing of course what his decision would be.

He said, with a new note of resolution: ''We have a full life ahead of us, then. Now that we — now that I can put this out of my mind. However much I may regret that it was ever allowed to enter — it *happened*. I cannot — no one ever can — withdraw the past. Elizabeth, I hav to say that I have been at fault in all this. Perhaps now — from now on . . . some of the unhappiness can be forgiven . . . the disagreeable times forgot.''

She squeezed his hand. ''Go and look at our daughter.''

He got up and moved over to the cot. In the shade of the cot, just out of range of the light of the fire flames, a small red face blinked its unfringed blue eyes, and the tiny mouth opened and closed. He put down a finger, and a hand no bigger than a soft pink walnut closed around it. He noted that she was much smaller than Valentine had been. But then Valentine had been an eight-month child.

He stood a while, swaying a little on the balls of his feet, not so much from inebriety as from the satisfaction that was flooding over him. He was moved. It was something very basic in his nature that resented the emotional strain put upon him by marriage and parenthood. A part of his character would have been far more ___nt with figures and commerce all day ___ Uncle Cary, not these terrible ___ war, these battlefields of sensation that plagued him on the level of his personal existence.

Yet because of them he was living more deeply, and when, as now, there was a gratifying outcome to it all . . . He went back to the bed.

"What shall we call her?"

Elizabeth opened her eyes.

"Ursula," she said without hesitation.

"Ursula?"

"Yes. You called him Valentine, so I think it is my turn. My godmother, who was also my great-aunt, was called Ursula. My great-uncle died when she was thirty and she lived as a widow for thirty-eight years."

"Ursula," said George, and tried it over on his tongue. "I would not quibble with that. But was there something especial — about your godmother?"

"I think she brought the brains into the Chynoweth family. That's if you think we have any! Though much older, she was a friend of Mary Wollstonecraft, and she translated books from the Greek."

"Ursula Warleggan. Yes, I am not at all unpartial to that. Valentine Warleggan

Ursula Warleggan. They would make a famous pair."

Through a haze of sleep Elizabeth noticed the pairing of the names with special satisfaction, and silently blessed Dr. Anselm for his assistance in bringing about such a result.

George knew it was time to go. But he had one more thing to say.

"Elizabeth."

"Yes?"

"Yesterday when I came, my visit was not without purpose. I had something to tell you."

"I hope it is good."

"Yes, it is good. You'll remember I called to see Mr. Pitt in the morning of the day before we left London."

". . . I knew you were going . . . But you did not tell me afterwards."

George grunted and turned the money in his fob. "No. Well, there was that reason. As you know. I trust it will never exist again. It is our duty to see that it ____ exists again . . . But I have to tell ____ that my interview with the ____ r was very agreeable and very useful. I gave him my promise of full support, and he was gracious enough to accept my expressions of loyalty."

". . . I'm glad."

"Well, that was three weeks ago. Yesterday morning I received a letter from John Robinson. He was able to tell me that Pitt has found it possible to agree to my request — my solitary and only request — and will be pleased to recommend to His Majesty that I receive a knighthood in the new year."

A faint breath of noise, like a tiny sigh, came from the infant in her cot, registering her first comment upon this strange new world.

Elizabeth opened her own eyes wide, those beautiful grey-blue eyes that had always fascinated him. "Oh, George, I am so *very* gratified!"

George smiled freely; a rare occurrence for him. "I suspected you would be — Lady Warleggan."

There was a light tap on the door. It was Lucy Pipe. "If ye plaise, sur, Dr. Behenna be downstairs. Shall 'e come up?"

"No. He shall not come up. First yo

921

mistress must sleep.'' The head hastily withdrew. George said: "You must sleep, my dear.'' His voice carried more warmth than had ever been heard in it before.

Elizabeth's eyes drooped. "Yes.''

"Sleep well, Lady Warleggan,'' George said, bending and kissing her.

"Thank you, Sir . . . Sir George.''

II

Dr. Behenna was not a little put out after his long and tiresome journey to be told that the child was already safely delivered and that mother and child were doing well. He was still more put out by George's refusal to allow him to see the patient. In most households he would of course have tramped straight up and into the bedroom; but with the Warleggans and their *nouveau riche* insistence on their own importance in the world he had to go more carefully.

And when Mr. Warleggan eventually descended to come down Mr. ...n was adamant. His wife had ...ully borne her child and now

922

must sleep. Miss Odgers was with her and would summon them if the need arose. George knew that Behenna was one of those men mentally incapable of tiptoeing into a bedroom, so for the time being he must be confined to the ground floor.

To assauge him he led him into the dining room, where the old Chynoweths were dozing over their brandy and port, and the kitchens were alerted to serve a late dinner for two hungry men.

Mrs. Chynoweth was naturally delighted to learn that she had a granddaughter, and like Dr. Behenna took umbrage that she was not immediately allowed upstairs. Mr. Chynoweth was too far gone to rejoice, and presently laid his head on the table and snored through the rest of the meal. It was a large table and they were able to eat at the other end.

George was never a great talker, and Dr. Behenna was still nursing his grievance, so the dominating voice at the table, often the only one, was the aristocratic but thick-tongued and slurred voice of the grandmother, Mrs. Joan Chynoweth — née Le Grice, as sh pointed out — one of the oldest and most distinguished families in England.

"Rubbish," Jonathan Chynoweth was heard to exclaim under his breath, having caught enough of this through his drunken doze. "Very or-ordinary sort of family. Came from Normandy only a couple of centuries ago. Very ordinary."

His wife went into lengthy speculations as to a suitable name for the child. George ate on, remembering the previous occasion, after Valentine was born, when there had been a similar conversation as to what *he* should be called. Only then it had been his own father who had been here; and curled in an armchair like an ancient crone, putting in her asp-like suggestions from time to time, had been that evil, festering harridan, Agatha Poldark.

George was not a superstitious man, but he recalled his mother's dread of the old woman; in an earlier age Agatha would have been one of the first to face the ducking stool and the fire. Well deserved, black succubus could have done harm him. Even his father's is had seemed to stem from that night when the fire had smoked as if the draught had been supernaturally reversed. He had been a cursed fool himself to have taken heed of the vile old woman. Even on the day of Valentine's birth she had pointed out that he had been born at a moon's eclipse and therefore would be unlucky all his life.

Of course from the very beginning she had hated George — before even he had begun to notice or to hate her. As the living embodiment of the four generations of Poldarks she had outlived, she had above all resented the arrival of this upstart — allowed here at first on sufferance because he was a school friend of Francis — she had witnessed his insignificance and gradual growth to significance: she had watched and come to detest his progress until he became first the owner of Francis and then the owner of this house. It had been just as intolerable for Agatha to witness as it had been stimulating and satisfying for George to experience.

Although the edge of pleasure wore blunter with repetition — as all pleasure did — he still knew the satisfaction of coming into this gracious Tudor manor house and gazing round and remembering his first visit here as a youth of eighteen, unpolished, unsophisticated, unlearned in the nicer manners. Then the Poldarks had seemed immeasurably superior to him, and immensely secure in their position and their property. Charles William, Francis's father, fat and impressive in his long vermilion coat, with his belches, his unstable humours, his patronising friendliness; and Charles William's widowed sister, Mrs. Johns; and *her* son and daughter-in-law, the Reverend and Mrs. Alfred Johns; and Francis's elder sister, Verity; and Ross, Francis's other cousin, the dark, quiet, difficult one, whom George had also known at school and had already learned to dislike; and the relative who was always absent, Ross's father, because he had got into so many disreputable scrapes that he was not mentioned in the house. Over them all Agatha had presided, half doyen, neglected maiden aunt, but ng some watchful spirit to which the family paid tribute.

Now all, all had gone. Verity to Falmouth, the Alfred Johnses to Plymouth, Ross to his own lair, the rest to the grave. And he, the rough unlearned youth, owned it all. As he now owned so much in Cornwall. But perhaps this estate was the property he valued most highly.

"Ursula," he said, thinking aloud.

"Eh?" said Mrs. Chynoweth. "Who? What do you say?"

"That is what she is to be called."

"The th-child? My granddaughter?"

"Elizabeth wishes it. And I like it well."

"Ursula," said Jonathan, raising himself an inch or two from the table. "Ursula. The little she-bear. Very good. I call that very good." He laid his head peaceably to rest.

Mrs. Chynoweth dabbed at her one good eye. "Ursula. That was the th-name of Morwenna's grandmother. She was Elizabeth's th-godmother. She died th-not so long ago."

George stiffened but did not say anything.

"Not that I cared for her so vastly," said Mrs. Chynoweth. "She thought th-too much about the rights of th-woman. My — my father once th-said — my father once th-said: 'If a woman do have blue stockings she must th-contrive that her petticoat shall hide 'em.' *She* didn't. She never — never hid them."

"I'll trouble you to pass me the mustard sauce," said Dr. Behenna.

"Why do you say 'the little she-bear'?" George asked Jonathan, but his father-in-law answered with a snore.

"I believe that is what the name means," said Dr. Behenna. "Do I understand, Mr. Warleggan, that you are offering me hospitality for the night?"

"The little she-bear," said George. "Well, I have no objection to that. And that name Ursula Warleggan runs very well." He looked coldly at the doctor. "What was that you said? Well, yes, of course. Naturally you shall stay the night. It is not a ride you would wish to ʈake in the dark, is it?"

ʌa bowed with equal lack of "Very well. But as I have so far been prevented from seeing my patient I wondered whether you wished to avail yourself of my services at all."

George said impatiently: "God's life, man! The child has been born scarce more than three hours. Dr. Enys gave my wife a draught and they are now both sleeping. Of course you may see them when they wake. Until then I would have thought it simple medical sense to allow them to rest."

"Indeed," said Behenna pettishly. "Just so."

"Even I have th-not been allowed to see them," said Mrs. Chynoweth. "And after all th-a grandmother should have certain rights. But th-dear Mr. Warleggan will decide . . . You decide most things, th-George, and upon my soul, that is the way it should be in a th-properly conducted th-household."

George reflected that it had never been so in his mother-in-law's household, where she had always held the reins over Jonathan. Nevertheless at Trenwith she had a proper view of the importance of her son-in-law in her world toda·

Without him they would both have long since mouldered away at their old home, Cusgarne; here they lived in comfort and idleness, warmed and fed and waited on, and would do so till they died. Mrs. Chynoweth had never been a woman to ignore the practical realities of a situation.

All the same, he well knew that Mrs. Chynoweth would once have been horrified at the thought of her beautiful young porcelain daughter forming anything so degrading as a union with the common Warleggan boy.

So time had moved on and values shifted and changed.

Elizabeth slept right through until after supper, when she woke feeling much refreshed, and all the people who were waiting to see her were permitted to see her. Ursula was also inspected and admired. Dr. Behenna restricted his examination to the briefest and professed himself satisfied. At midnight they all retired to rest. At three A.M. Dr. Behenna was awakened by Ellen Prowse, who told him her mistress was suffering severe pains in the arms and legs.

CHAPTER XV

It was not until the Thursday morning that George sent for Dwight. Caroline, feeling neighbourly, was at that time just pinning on a hat to call on Elizabeth and admire the baby. She now unpinned it and let Dwight go alone.

Dr. Behenna was with George in the hall, but they were not speaking to each other.

George was pale and had not slept. "Mrs. Warleggan is in great pain and has been now for thirty-six hours. I should be glad if you will go up and see if you can aid her."

Dwight looked at Behenna, who said stiffly: "The premature labour has brought on an acute gouty condition of the abdominal viscera which is manifesting itself in severe cramp-like spasms of th extremities. All that can be done is being done, but Mr. Warleggan feels that, since you delivered the child, you should be brought in for further consultation."

Dwight nodded. "What have you prescribed?"

"Some bleeding. Infusion of the leaves of *Atropa belladonna*. Salt of wormwood and ammoniac. Light purges to reduce the excessive pressure of the nerve fluids." Behenna spoke with keen annoyance — one did not usually give away the details of one's treatments to a rival — and Dwight was surprised that he was being so frank.

An old woman came out of one of the rooms and limped across the hall; Dwight hardly recognised her as Mrs. Chynoweth.

He said to Behenna: "Would you lead the way, sir?"

When he got in the bedroom Dwight stared at Elizabeth in horror. She had aged ten years, and her face was thin and etched with pain. Dwight sniffed slightly ame into the room. Then he went d.

Warleggan. This is a sad change.

We must get you well soon."

"Of course we will get her well soon!" Behenna was right behind him. He despised doctors who let their patients know how ill they looked. "A few days and you will be about again."

"Now tell me, what is it? Where is your pain?"

Elizabeth moistened her lips to speak, and could not. She stared up at Dwight. Dwight bent his head close to her mouth. She said: "My — feet. All my body — *aches* — I have never felt so ill — or felt such *pain*." Her tongue, he saw, was swollen and coated with a dark reddish stain of blood.

"You have given her opiates?" Dwight asked Behenna.

"Some, yes. But it is more important at this stage to increase the elasticity of the veins and to clear the effete matter rioting in the bloodstream."

"So *cold*," whispered Elizabeth.

Dwight glanced at the fire blazing in the hearth. Lucy Pipe was sitting beside it gently stirring the cot. He put his hand on Elizabeth's brow and then felt her pulse,

933

which was very rapid. The fingers of one hand were blue and swollen.

He said: "Perhaps I might examine you, Mrs. Warleggan. I will try not to hurt you."

He pulled the bedclothes gently back and pressed light fingers on her abdomen. She winced and groaned. Then he pulled the sheet further back and looked at her feet. He closed his hand on the right foot. Then he looked at the left foot. Then he stroked each leg up as far as the knee.

He straightened up and the bedclothes were put back. He knew now why Dr. Behenna had been so frank about the details of his treatments. They were doing no good.

A faint cry came from the cot.

He snapped: "Get that child out of here!"

"Oh," said Elizabeth, suddenly more alert. "Oh, why? Why? Why?"

"Because you must have perfect rest and quiet," Dwight said gently. "Even the smallest noise must not disturb you."

George had come into the room and was staring down at his wife with a concentrated frown of one who fears he is being bested at some game of which he does not know the rules.

"Well?" he said.

Dwight bit his lip. "First I will give you something stronger to ease the pain, Mrs. Warleggan. Dr. Behenna is correct in supposing it to be a condition of the blood. He and I must work together to help alleviate this condition."

"What is the cure for it?" George demanded.

Dwight said: "We must take one step at a time, Mr. Warleggan. Let us aim first at the alleviation. Afterwards we can attempt — the rest. I shall give her a strong opiate at once, and then we must try to bring greater warmth to the limbs. But in the gentlest possible way. Are you thirsty?"

"All . . . all the time."

"Then lemonade — as much as she can drink. She must have warm bricks to her feet and her hands rubbed lightly. But only *warm* bricks, changed hourly. Above all we must try to restore her body heat. It is of the utmost urgency. I want the fire built up and the window a little open.

You will be staying, Dr. Behenna?"

"I have patients in town, but they must wait."

Dwight smiled at Elizabeth. "Have patience, ma'am, we will try to help you as quick as possible." He turned. "Then we must wait, Mr. Warleggan. There is nothing more we can do at this stage. Dr. Behenna, may I have the favour of a word with you in private?"

Behenna grunted and inclined his head. The two men went off into Elizabeth's dressing room, with its pretty pink hangings and elegant lace table covers.

Behenna shut the door: "Well?"

Dwight said: "I take it you don't *believe* this to be a gouty condition at all?"

Behenna grunted. "The excessive excitability of the nerve fluids suggests a severe gouty inflammation which may well predispose towards the symptoms we are now observing."

Dwight said: "You have clearly not ever been in a prisoner-of-war camp, sir."

"What do you mean by that?"

Dwight hesitated again. He dreaded

even formulating the words. "Well, it appears plain to me. Can you not smell anything?"

"I must agree there is a very slight disturbing odour which I did not notice until this forenoon. But that . . ."

"Yes, *that*. Though God in His heaven only knows what may have brought her to such a condition!"

"Are you suggesting, sir, that my treatment is in some way responsible?"

"I am suggesting nothing — "

"I could as well suggest to you, sir, that had I been here to deliver the child this condition might not have supervened!"

Dwight looked at the other man.

"We're both physicians, Dr. Behenna, and I believe equally dedicated to the succour and cure of human ills. Our treatments may differ as widely as two languages, but our aims are similar and our integrity, I trust, is not in question. So I'd suggest to you that there is nothing I could have done in delivering a child in an uncomplicated birth, or anything you could have done in prescribing the treatments that you have described to me, which would or could produce the symptoms Mrs. Warleggan is now suffering from."

Behenna paced about.

"Agreed."

Dwight said: "Contraction of the arteries, restricting and then inhibiting the blood supply. This is what appears to be occurring. Particularly and most dangerously restricting the blood supply to the limbs. There appears to be no *reason* for it! The birth, as I have told you, was unexceptional: premature but otherwise only distinguished by the fact that the uterine spasms were very rapid and over-emphatic. But I took that to be a characteristic of the patient — after all, a woman I delivered last week gave birth to a child in fifty-five minutes from having complained of the first pains. It was that, I thought, or an outcome of the fall she had had and not indicating any pathological complications. Now this . . . the cause is obscure; the disease hardly so."

Behenna said: "You're going too fast and too far." He glanced at Enys.

"I pray I am. Indeed I do. We shall know soon enough."

"I trust you do not intend to publish your suspicion to Mr. Warleggan."

"Far from it. In the meantime, though you may doubt my diagnosis you do not, I trust, disassociate yourself from my treatment?"

"No . . . It can do no harm."

II

Ross was in Truro all day Friday, the thirteenth, attending his second meeting at the Cornish Bank as a partner and guarantor. The duel was not mentioned, though everyone must have known about it for the simple reason that no one remarked on the stiffness of his right hand. Movement was returning, but he still had difficulty in signing his name.

For the most part the talk was double Dutch to him, though he maintained a polite attention. On matters of broad policy he found he was of some general use, and, although Lord de Dunstanville must have had many other ears to the ground in London, Ross was the only member of Parliament present and could contribute here and there.

After it was over he supped and slept with Harris Pascoe in Calenick, where for the moment he was continuing to live with his sister. The old premises of Pascoe's Bank would be sold or pulled down, and Harris was looking for a smaller house in Truro, near the centre, whence he could walk daily to the new bank. He had fitted well into his reorganised life, and although he lacked the prestige of being entirely his own man, he was saved much of the anxiety, and, as he said to Ross in his usual deprecating way, this was no bad thing for someone of his age and disposition.

Ross left on the Saturday morning and was home by midday. It was the darkest day of the year, of the whole winter, for although no rain fell the world was sunk in cloud, and dawn and dusk were nominal terms to indicate grudging changes is visibility.

As soon as he got home Demelza told him she had heard Elizabeth was still gravely ill. They had heard yesterday through Caroline, and Demelza had been to Killewarren this morning to inquire.

"It was the nearest I could go," she said. "If we were neighbours in any proper sense . . ."

"Did she say there was any change at all?"

"Not for the better. Dwight was at Trenwith then."

"Is the child alive?"

"Oh, yes, and well, I believe. Premature but well."

They met each other's eyes but said no more.

Dinner was usually taken with the children, and, now that Mrs. Kemp was becoming something of a permanent resident, with her too; so there was no lack of talk. Clowance, from being a silent child, was now vying with Jeremy in an ability to keep up a nonstop conversation whether anyone was listening or not.

Ross did not eat much, and halfway through the meal he said in an undertone to Demelza: "I think I must go."

Demelza nodded. "I think you should.

Only I'm afraid for you."

"I can look to myself."

"If you were to meet Tom Harry in the grounds — and you with your weak arm."

"He could not stop me on a horse. And at a time like this George must surely admit me."

"I . . . wouldn't rely on it, Ross."

"No." Ross bethought himself of their last meeting. "I can only try."

"Should I come?"

"No . . . If there have to be insults I can swallow them, on such an occasion as this. But if you were insulted I could not."

"Take Gimlett with you."

"I don't think he would terrify a mouse. Tholly Tregirls is the man, but I can hardly draw him out of his kiddley just to accompany me on a social call."

"A sick visit," said Demelza.

"Whichever you say . . . I think I'll go now, while the daylight lasts — such as it is."

Demelza said: "I'll light the candles."

To the accompaniment of a dozen

questions Ross got up and went for his cloak and hat. As he left he kissed Demelza, which was unusual for him in midafternoon.

She said: "Don't stay too long, or I shall worry. For your safety, I mean."

He smiled. "For my safety."

Outside he cast a glance at the sea, which had now lost all its wildness. It was coming in like an oilcloth that was being lifted by a draught, only the edges frayed with dirty white. Sea gulls were celebrating the darkness of the day.

When he turned in at the gates of Trenwith a number of lights already flickered in the building. Few houses, he thought, responded more quickly to mood than Trenwith. When he had been here on that summer evening eighteen months ago it had been pulsating and gay; now it looked still and cold, as cold as the Christmas when he had visited Aunt Agatha.

There were no gamekeepers about. He dismounted and knocked on the door. It was opened almost immediately by a manservant he did not know.

"Are you the — oh . . ."

Ross said: "I came to inquire about Mrs. Warleggan. Is Mr. Warleggan in?"

"Mrs. Warleggan . . . Well . . ."

"My name is Poldark."

"Oh . . ." The man seemed frozen.

"What is it?" said a voice behind. It was George.

His face was in the shadow but his voice was at its coldest.

Ross said: "I come in peace, George. I come simply to inquire after Elizabeth. I trust she's better."

There were noises inside the house but it was difficult to identify them.

George said: "Turn this man away."

"I came to ask how she was," Ross said. "That is all. I think at times of sickness one should be able to set aside old feuds — even the bitterest of feuds."

George said: "Turn this man away."

The door was shutting. Ross put his foot in it and his good shoulder against it and shoved. The manservant staggered back and collided with a table. Ross went in. There was only single candle guttering in the great hall. It looked like a wobbling yellow eye in the iron-grey daylight.

Ross shut the door behind him. "For *God's* sake, George! Have we to be so petty as to quarrel like mangy dogs at a time of *sickness?* Tell me she is better. Tell me she is about the same. Tell me what the doctors say, and I will *go!* And go gladly! I have no business here but that of a long-standing relationship with this house, and those in it. I am related by marriage to Elizabeth, and wish her only well . . ."

George said: "God damn you, and your family, and your blood to all eternity." He choked and stopped as if he was ill himself.

Ross waited, but no more came. The manservant had recovered himself and was rearranging the table he had upset.

Ross said: "I will not go till I know how she is."

"Elizabeth?" said George. "Oh, Elizabeth? . . . Elizabeth is dead."

III

In the silence that followed, the manservant slid away silently and was gone from the hall.

The hall itself was like a church, echoing and cold; sickly light from the multi-paned window falling upon the great table, the empty hearth; and the one candle burning.

Ross said: "It . . . you can't . . ." He took a breath. "She can't . . ."

"Two hours ago," said George in a detached voice; "she died, holding my hand. Is that any pleasure to you?"

Ross recognised now the sound he had heard earlier. It was someone crying, a woman, almost a wail, like a Celtic keening. No one would have recognised Mrs. Chynoweth, whose voice for some years had been muffled and halting.

"Elizabeth is . . . I can't — believe . . . George, this is not some . . ."

"Some jest?" said George. "Oh, yes, I jest from time to time, but not on such a trivial subject as the loss of a wife."

Ross stood as if his limbs were unable

to make any concerted movement. He licked his lips and stared at the other man.

"Go on, you scum!" George shouted. "Go up and *see* her! See what we have brought her to!"

A man came out of the winter parlour. At another time Ross would have recognised him as Dr. Behenna.

"Mr. Warleggan, I beg of you not to upset yourself further. No more could have been done, and there is nothing to do now — "

George turned. "I have Captain Poldark here. Captain Poldark, M.P. He doubts my word that my wife — whom he long coveted — is dead. He thinks I am jesting. I have invited him to go up and see."

"Mr. Warleggan, if I might suggest — "

"Where is she?"

George looked at Ross. "In the pink bedroom overlooking the courtyard. You must know your way about this house, since you have always felt it belonged to you. Go up and see her for yourself.

There is no one with her. No one will stay with her."

"Captain Poldark — " Behenna began, but Ross was already making for the stairs.

He went up them, stumbling here and there. It was dark in the interior of the house, and another solitary candle burned at the end of the long passage. Past Verity's old bedroom, past Francis's bedroom, past Aunt Agatha's bedroom. Shadows barred his way. He stumbled against an ancient tallboy. The floorboards creaked under his tread. Past the bedroom where he and Demelza had once slept and made love. Up five steps. Those five steps that Elizabeth had fallen down before the birth of Valentine.

He came to the door. He could not bring himself to open it. It was the room in which he had come to see Elizabeth seven years ago — a meeting from which so much mischief had sprung. Suddenly as a non-believer and a non-Catholic he wanted to cross himself.

He opened the door, and the stench hit him like a wall.

The bed was there, and Elizabeth was on it, and two candles burned. The fire still flickered in the grate.

The curtains were drawn but a window was slightly open. The only movement in the room was a stirring of the pink curtain in the evening breeze. On the table by the bed were an hourglass, a bowl, a tall painted feeding bottle, two lemons. On the dressing table was Elizabeth's necklace of garnets, a glass containing three leeches, a pair of scissors, and a bottle of water and a spoon. Before the fire were her slippers, and a kettle hissed faintly on the hob.

He hung on to the handle of the door and retched. She did not move to greet him.

He retched again and again, and pulled out a handkerchief and put it to his nose and mouth. He stared at his first love. The candles dipped in the draught of the open door.

He walked slowly to the bed. Death had removed all the lines of pain and fatigue and fever. Except that her skin was yellow. Her hair, unbrushed but curiously tidy, still framed that pale patrician face.

Robbed of expression, her face in repose retained the old sweet beauty so many men had admired. You could have supposed that at any moment her eyelids would flicker open and her lips would curve into a welcoming smile. Except that her skin was yellow.

And under the sheet, and barely contained by it, lay all the horrors of corruption, mortification, and decay. It was creeping up by every minute that she lay there. How far had it already reached? She had decayed while still alive, so that burial was already days overdue.

He swallowed back vomit, and took the handkerchief from his mouth and kissed her. Her lips were like soft cold stale putty.

Handkerchief back, he heaved his heart out against it and almost fell. The room swung as he caught at a chair. He turned and fled. The bang of the door behind him sounded hollow; the door of a sepulchre. A sepulchre that needed sealing off from all that was still alive.

He reeled along the passage and down the stairs without looking at George, who stood there watching him. He went out of the house and found his horse, and leaned his head against the horse's neck, unable to mount.

IV

George said: "Tell me the sum I am in your debt and I will pay you."

"In due course. I'll attend to it in due course."

"Let me know when you want your horse brought from the stables."

"As it is again night," Dr. Behenna said stiffly, "I should prefer to sleep here. Also, I think it advisable to look at the baby once more before I go."

"She's not unwell?"

"Not at all. But I am not sure if the wet nurse is not a thought clumsy. These country girls . . ."

"She was the best to be found at such short notice."

"Oh, quite. I've given Mrs. Chynoweth a strong opiate, and she should sleep sound now. The women are upstairs now?"

"The women are upstairs."

"I think the casque should be closed as quick as possible."

"I'm sure they will feel the same."

Somewhere in a nearby room Valentine was arguing with his nurse. He did not yet know anything except that Mama was unwell.

George went prowling round the cold shadowy silent house. This thing that had happened to him was contrary to all his previous experiences of life. In forty years he had suffered few setbacks, and they had all been man-made and capable of reversal. Most of them *had* been reversed in the fulness of time. One accepted a rebuff, a defeat, and then carefully gauged the size and quality of the defeat and set one's mind to arranging future events in such a way as to overcome or circumvent it. Of course from time to time he and his parents had had minor or more than minor ailments, and one accepted that in due course one would grow old and die. But in forty years he had not *lost* anybody — certainly nobody important.

This total defeat was something he

found difficult — impossible — to accept. From the age of twenty Elizabeth had been his goal — for long quite out of reach, beyond all possibility of attainment. But he had attained her, against all probability, against all the odds. This had been his greatest triumph. Since then, though he had allowed suspicion and jealousy to rage in him and impair his life with her, it had been rage against his *own,* it had been bitter anger within a circumscribed area of personal possession. So when on the rare occasions jealousy had broken into bitter quarrel, he had been prepared to back down at the last under her threat to leave him. He might be miserable *with* her, and fiercely intent on making her life miserable too, but there had never been any question in his mind that he was ever going to be *without* her.

For she was the person he had been working for — to please, to offend, to observe, to criticise, to consult, even to insult, to show off to others, to buy things for, above all to *impress. There was nobody else.* And now, and now when

Aunt Agatha's spleen had just lost its venom, when the poison barb had at last been withdrawn and they could live in a greater amity together, when they had a *daughter* to add to their son, when life could really begin anew, when — *especially* — he was on the point of achieving that ultimate pinnacle of distinction, a knighthood — he, George Warleggan, the blacksmith's grandson — a knighthood — Sir George . . . Sir George and Lady Warleggan . . . coming into a reception . . . everyone would look — one of the wealthiest men in Cornwall and one of the most influential, member of Parliament, owner of a parliamentary borough, and a *knight;* and on his arm the fair-haired gracious aristocratic Elizabeth: Lady Warleggan . . . and at this stage she had been *snatched away.*

It was not *bearable.* He stared around him at the room he found himself in — it was a guest room and he did not know why he had come in here. It was next to Agatha's old room, and he quickly went out and entered hers. She had cursed him, she had *cursed* him! — all this time her curse had lain on him, and now, when he had been about to cast it off, she had cursed him afresh, and his life was laid waste.

Most of the furniture was unchanged from when she had died — this was the bed she had died on. He kicked violently at the dressing table, splintering one of the legs. Then he pushed it over and it fell with a crash, smashing the glass and scattering toiletries about the floor. He wrenched open the door of the wardrobe and tugged at it. Slowly it toppled and fell with a resounding thud, bringing over a chair and breaking a wooden table in its fall. The candle he had brought in lurched on its shelf and nearly fell too.

This was a cursed house, and he would willingly have burned it down — the candle to the curtain and to the corner of the bedspread — there was plenty of ancient timber which would soon ignite: a fitting pyre for Elizabeth and all the cursed and twice damned Poldarks who had ever lived here.

But in spite of his insensate anger it was not in him, not in his nature to destroy property, especially property which more than ever now was by rights his. He stared around the room, his hands still trembling with passion, and tore off the walls two pictures which had belonged to Agatha, dashed them to the floor. He thought tomorrow night — or perhaps even tonight — he would go to Sawle Church and desecrate her grave — have two men smash the headstone, dig up the rotten powdered corpse and *throw* it around and *throw* it around for the crows to pick. Anything, anything, to revenge himself for this unrevengeable injury he had suffered.

He tremblingly took up the candle again and went out of the room, dripping tallow on his fingers and all over the floor. He stood outside, unable to contain his anger yet unable to find a subject on which to vent it. He would have gone again in to see Elizabeth, but knew it was better to wait until the two women had finished laying her out and the room had been heavily scattered with chloride of lime. He did not know whether he could bear to go in even then.

She had left him. She had *left* him. He

couldn't *believe* it.

He could not tolerate the thought of returning to the rooms downstairs where he might encounter that inept quack, Behenna, or, worse, Elizabeth's doddering, feeble-faced father. If he saw him he would cry: why are *you* alive? What good are *you* to me? Why don't you and your miserable wife die too?

A girl had come out of a door and was staring at him. It was Polly Odgers.

"Beg pardon, sir. I didn't rightly know if anything was wrong . . . I mean *more* wrong. I heard those noises — crashes and the like. I didn't rightly know what they were."

"Nothing," he said between his teeth. "It is nothing."

"Oh . . . Thank you, sir. Excuse me." She prepared to withdraw.

"Did it wake the child?"

"Oh, no, sir; she's a proper little sleeper. And hungry with it! She's grown, I believe she's grown in just four days!"

He followed her into the room. Mrs. Simons, the young wet nurse, bobbed him a curtsy as he came in.

He stared down at the child. Ursula Warleggan. But Elizabeth had left him. This was all that was left. She had left him Ursula.

He stayed motionless for a long time, and the two young women watched him, careful not to disturb his thoughts.

He had held her hand while she was dying. When Behenna said there was no more hope, he had come into the loathsome, nauseous room and sat down beside her and held her hand. One hand was badly swollen but the other as pale and slim as ever. He had thought her unconscious, but her fingers had moved in his. It was her left hand, and his ring was on it, his ring proclaiming his pride and his capture, which he had put on her finger in the dilapidated old church of Mylor by the river Fal less than seven years ago. With what pride and triumph. And now it had come to this.

Once towards the end she had come round and tried to smile at him through her parched and discoloured lips. Then the smile had disappeared and a look of dread had come over her face. "George," she had whispered. "it's going dark! I'm afraid of the dark." He had held her hand more tightly as if with his firm grip he could keep her in this world, hold her against the drag of all the horrors that drew her to the grave.

He thought of all this, standing staring down at the child which was all Elizabeth had left him. He was no philosopher and no seer, but had he been both he might have wondered at the fact that his fair-haired, frailly beautiful wife had now borne three children and that none of them would come to resemble her at all. Though Elizabeth had been constitutionally strong enough, perhaps some exhaustion in the ancient Chynoweth strain was to be the cause of this virtual obliteration of her personal appearance in any of her children, and the dominance of the three fathers. Geoffrey Charles was already like Francis. Valentine would grow ever more like the man who had just left the house. And little Ursula would become sturdy and strong and thick-necked and as determined as a blacksmith.

The child stirred in her sleep; still so

tiny; still so frail. "Look after the children," Elizabeth had whispered. Very well, very well: he would do that; but what was the use of *that?* It was his *wife* he wanted: the person you did things *for,* the cornerstone. All his labour, all his scheming, all his organising and amassing and negotiating and achieving . . . without her it was all in *vain.* He could have kicked this cot over like the furniture in Agatha's room; turned it upside down with its frail contents, as his life had been overset, killed, made empty by a solitary stroke of malignant fate. He blamed fate, never knowing that he should have blamed himself.

Polly Odgers leaned forward and pulled a corner of the blanket further from the child's mouth. "Dear of'n," she said.

"Ursula," George muttered. "The little she-bear."

"Please?"

"Nothing," said George.

And for the first time he had to take a handkerchief to wipe his eyes.

CHAPTER XVI

Ross walked home beside his horse. Shock and horror had made his limbs so weak that to go home slowly step by step with Sheridan beside him was more instinct than choice.

He walked through Grambler village and past Sawle Church out onto the moorland. A wind was soughing over the land.

This was the most familiar way in the world to him; he had run from one house to the other in childhood and in boyhood; he had ridden this way and walked this way more times than he could estimate. But it was Sheridan who knew the path tonight.

One or two people passed and called good night. It was a Cornish custom, not always mere friendliness but often curiosity to identify the other in the dark. Tonight he did not reply. The horror was on him. As a soldier he had seen enough, but this was different. That she should have decayed like that while still looking so beautiful was something he would never be able to rid himself of. This was what love came to. This was what beauty came to. The worm. God in Christ!

He shuddered and spat. The sickness lay in his stomach like the gangrene she had died of.

He came up to the Meeting House beside Wheal Maiden. There was a light in it. Probably Sam. Perhaps a few faithful members of the class praying or listening to him read. Perhaps he should go in, kneel in a corner, ask for guidance and pray for humility. That was what all men lacked. Humility and perspective. But the latter was dangerous. With perspective one could always perceive the end.

Something moved. "Is it you, Ross?"

"Demelza," he said. "What are you doing here?"

"I thought to come this far — just to watch for you . . . Why are you walking?"

"I — wished to take my time."

She said: "I know what's happened. Caroline sent Myners over to tell us."

"I'm glad you know."

They turned and began to walk back. She said: "I'm that sorry."

He said: "Let us not talk about it."

They went down the valley. As soon as they reached home she went in and hustled the children out of the parlour, and he sat before the fire and drank the brandy she brought. She helped him off with his boots.

"Do you want to be alone?"

"Not if you'll stay."

So she told the children to be quiet in the kitchen, and fetched her sewing and took a chair on the other side of the fire. He drank brandy for about an hour. She had a couple of small glasses. At last he looked up.

"I'm sorry," he said.

"Do you want supper?"

"*No*. No food. But take some yourself. Are the children in the dining room?"

"I don't know. I'm not that hungry."

"It's been a dark day," he said.

"Sometimes I think there are days in December when the human spirit is at its lowest. This is such a one."

"With good reason. Did she — "

"I'd — rather not talk about it."

They sat for about another hour. He had stopped drinking but lay back dozing, with his head against the back of the high chair. She went out and said good night to the children and cut herself a piece of bread and cheese.

When she went in again he said: "I think I'll go for a walk."

"At this time?"

"Yes . . . it might help. Don't wait up."

"You don't want for me to come with you, then?"

"I think I shall go too far."

She said: "Remember to come back."

When he got out the three-quarter moon was rising, invisible and smothered in cloud, but lightening the way. He went on to Hendrawna Beach, where the tide was far out, and began to walk across it. The sand broke under his weight, as crisp as frost. His own shadow, vague as a ghost, moved about his feet.

He went the way Drake had walked in his tribulation some months ago, but at the Holy Well he deserted the beach and climbed the rocky steps beside it till he reached the old path that the pilgrims had used centuries ago. Up and down, skirting the sandhills, with the sea murmuring just below, he stumbled on, passing the Dark Cliffs and Ellenglaze, skirted Hoblyn's Cove and dipped into the valley beyond. Except for the solitary crofter or gypsy, this was empty land, wind-swept and sand-swept, barren of vegetation except the marram grass and a few patches of gorse and heather. Not a tree. It was years since he had come this way. He did not remember ever having come this way since he returned from America sixteen years ago. There was nothing to come for. Except when, as now, he was trying to escape from himself.

Once or twice he sat down, not so much to rest as to think; but as soon as he began to think he was up and off again. As the night progressed so the sky lightened, and now and then the moon appeared, veiled and warped and wasted with age. The cliff edges became sharper, like the face of old men as the flesh shrinks from them. In some of the smaller, darker coves seaweed slithered on the rocks and stank of the sea's decay.

It was hours before he turned about and began the long tramp back. By now it was a question of making his tired body take over from his tired mind. Or accommodate his conscious thinking to ideas only of muscular effort. Back on the beach at last, he lengthened his stride to beat the tide as it came in. He rounded the Wheal Leisure cliffs with water splashing above his knees.

Day was just creeping up into the sky as he sighted Nampara. It came reluctantly, like someone drawing back the curtains in a shrouded room. Fine rain was beginning to fall. He found his way over the familiar stile, into the garden, past the lilac tree, and let himself into the house. He moved silently into the parlour, chilled with the sea water clammy about his legs and thinking some remnants of the fire might still be warm.

The fire was still in, though low, and

as he crouched before it someone stirred in his armchair. He stared and then saw who it was.

He said: "I *told* you. You should have gone to bed."

She said: "Why should I?"

They stayed in silence for a time, while he put pieces of coal on the fire and then used the bellows to blow it up.

"Are you cold?" he asked.

"Yes. Are you?"

He nodded and went to open the curtains. The sickly daylight showed that she had not undressed but had a blanket over her knees and a wrap round her shoulders.

"Let me get you some breakfast."

He shook his head. "You have something."

"No, no; I'm not hungry." She stirred. "You're wet."

"No matter. I'll change in a while." He poured himself a glass of brandy to try to take the stale taste of other brandy from his mouth. He offered her one but she refused.

"Have you been walking all night?"

"Yes. I think these boots are nearly through." He pulled them off, crouched again by the fire. She watched the warmer light play on his features. The brandy went down, burning deep. He made a face, and shivered. "Have you been asleep?"

"Sort of."

"But waiting."

"Waiting."

He subsided against the back of the other chair. "This is the end of the century, you know. It seems — appropriate. In a few weeks it will be eighteen hundred."

"I know."

"For perhaps very good reasons, it seems just now to be the end of more than the century to me. It seems to be the end of life as we've known it."

"Because of — Elizabeth's death?"

He baulked at the word. "Not altogether. Though that, of course."

"Do you want to talk about it now?"

"No — if you don't mind."

There was silence.

She said: "Well, the end of the century

does not mean the end of our lives, Ross."

"Oh . . . it's a fit of the deepest depression I am in. It will look different in a month or two. I'll recover by and by."

"There's no hurry."

"Perhaps there's always hurry."

He shovelled more coal on, and a puff of smoke blew into the room.

She said: "Go and sleep before the children wake."

"No. I want to talk to you, Demelza. What I've been thinking. Not long ago you lost someone you — loved. It — bites deep."

"Yes," she said. "It bites deep."

"Yet . . ." He reached for the brandy and then put it in the fireplace untasted. "Though I once loved Elizabeth, it's been the *memory* of that love that bit deepest tonight. Sometime this month or next I shall be forty. So there's always hurry. It is the memory — and the fear — of the loss of *all* love that bites deepest."

"I don't quite see what you mean."

"Well, in some ways my grief is a

selfish grief. Perhaps that's what Sam preaches. One can attain no goodness without subduing the self.''

''And do you wish to do that?''

''It's not what one wishes, it's what one should do.''

''Self . . .'' said Demelza. ''Is there no difference between self and selfishness? Is there no difference between — appreciating all the good things of life and — and exploiting the good things for one's own advantage? I think so.''

He stared at her with her dark hair falling carelessly about her shoulders, and under the wrap her canary silk frock, and her hands never quite still, and her breast rising and falling, and the dark vivid intelligence in her eyes.

He said: ''What I have seen last night — makes me sick at heart — sick for all the charm and beauty that is lost — in Elizabeth. But most of all it makes me afraid.''

''Afraid, Ross? What of?''

''Of losing you, I suppose.''

''There's little chance.''

''I don't mean to another man —

though that was bad enough. I mean just of losing you physically, as a person, as a companion, as a human presence being beside me and with me all my life."

Her heart opened to him. "Ross," she said, "there's no *chance*. Unless you throw me out."

"It's not a chance, it's a *certainty*," he said. "Seeing Elizabeth like that . . . We are at the end of a century, at the end of an era . . ."

"It's just a date."

"No, it isn't. Not for us. Not for anybody; but especially not for us. It's — it's a watershed. We have come up so far; now we look down."

"We look onwards, surely."

"Onwards and down. D'you realise there will come a time, there will *have* to come a time, when I shall never hear your voice again, or you mine? It may be sentimental to say so, but this — this fact is something I find intolerable, unthinkable, beyond bearing . . ."

Demelza moved from her chair suddenly, knelt to the fire and picked up the bellows and began to work them. It was to disguise the tears that had lurched to the edge of her lashes. She realised that he had reached some ultimate darkness of the soul, that he struggled in deep waters, and that perhaps only she could stretch out a hand.

"Ross, you mustn't be afraid. It's not like you. Tisn't in your nature."

"Perhaps one's nature changes as one grows older."

"It mustn't."

He watched her. "Aren't you ever afraid?"

"Yes. Oh, yes. Maybe every moment of the day if I allowed myself to think. But you can't *live,* not what way, if you think like that. I'm here. You're here. The children are upstairs. That's all that matters at this moment, at this time. The — the blood is in my veins. It's in yours. Our hearts beat. Our eyes see. Our ears hear. We smell and talk and feel."

She turned and squatted beside him on the carpet, and he put his arm round her, staring sightlessly into the dark.

She said: "And we're together. Isn't that important?"

"Even when it is like it was in London?"

"That mustn't ever be again."

"No," he said. "That mustn't ever be again."

"Of course there has to be an end," she said. "Of course. For that is what everyone has faced since the world began. And that is — what do you call it? — intolerable. It's intolerable! So you must not think of it. You must not face it. Because it is a — certainty it has to be forgotten. One cannot — must not — fear a certainty. All we know is this moment, and this moment, Ross, we are *alive!* We *are. We* are. The past is over, gone. What is to come doesn't exist yet. That's tomorrow! It's only now that can ever be, at any one moment. And at this moment, *now,* we are alive and together. We can't ask more. There isn't any more to ask."

Graham, Winston
Angry tide. Large print
ed. Volume 2

Date Due

1/80 mld		
6/51 wk		
2/62 JCC		